An Unconventional Love Affair

Brianne Turner

Published by Brianne Turner, 2024.

AN UNCONVENTIONAL LOVE AFFAIR

First edition. May 2, 2024.

Copyright © 2024 Brianne Turner.

ISBN: 979-8218304416

Written by Brianne Turner.

Table of Contents

Gianna

I hear my roommate's blasting music in the apartment. I groggily roll over, my eyes focusing on the alarm clock, its glowing numbers showing that it's 5am. With a sigh, I grab my pillow and cover my face, blocking out the world around me. I love my roommates, but sometimes they can be inconsiderate. I closed my eyes and tried to get at least 1 more hour before leaving for my shift. I hear a loud clang, showing that one of them is starting breakfast. Giving up, I got up and headed out to the kitchen.

"Good morning, Gigi; I'm making pancakes and sausage; you want some?" My roommate Jesse grins as she takes out the pans and bowls.

"You know I usually wake up at 8am because I don't have to leave for work until 9am" I sit in one of the bar chairs near the counter.

"Oh, I'm sorry that I woke you up. I woke early to get ahead on my teacher's plan for next month." I know she means well, but I'm not a morning person, but at least she cooks breakfast.

My other roommate, Rosie, comes out of her room dressed in her workout gear. "Good morning, ladies; anyone up to joining me for a workout?" She bounces to the fridge to make her pre-workout shake.

I grunt. "How do you find the energy to work out in the morning? " I put my head down on the counter, and Rosie and Jesse laughed.

Rosie smiles. "You know, working out in the morning does wonders for mental health," Jessie looks up as she mixes the pancake batter.

"I'm a weekend workout person," they chuckle.

Rosie comes around and hugs me from behind. "I'll be done with my workout in 40 minutes; love y'all" she presses the elevator button and gets in once it arrives. I realized I had left my phone on my bedside table and got up to get it and headed back to my seat. Scrolling through my notifications, I saw my Dad had texted me he'd bought me a ticket home for the weekend and sent money for my rent this month. I also saw a notification from a guy I met on Tinder that I've been seeing for a month. I open the text message, and it reads,

Tinder Guy: *Gigi, this past month has been incredible, but I don't see this turning into a relationship; we can still hook up.*

I take a deep breath; the nerves of some guys. That text doesn't deserve a response.

Jesse looks up from the stove. "Everything alright, Gigi?"

I huff. "Just another Tinder guy texting me. He doesn't want a relationship, but still wants to hook up. What goes through a man's head to assume I would be fine being a booty call after saying I'm not relationship material?"

Jesse shrugs. "I've been with my boyfriend since we were in high school," "you're lucky to be with someone faithful to you for 10 years." Jesse flips the pancake. "You will find your other half, eventually." She turns the sausage in the pan.

"I make it obvious on my profile, showing that I am dating to marry and settle down. I'm 28 and know I want to be married and have kids, but I think men and women get spooked when I tell them that."

Jesse plates my breakfast and hands it to me, and we head to our dining room to eat. "Most people aren't ready to settle down too young, so you might have to date around until you find that person. In the meantime, you can stay here with Rosie and me." I laugh, and we continue to eat and talk; when we are done, we clean up, and I head to my room to get ready.

I plugged in my phone, showered, and did my hair. Frustrated with my hair, I quickly tied it back to avoid any further annoyance. I picked out a Seattle Sounders jersey and my dark-wash jeans. It's Friday, so the call center is lax with the dress code, which is ridiculous because we are adults and should be able to govern ourselves. I checked the time and saw it was still 7 am, and I had another hour before I had to leave. I called my dad, and he picked up the first ring.

"Good morning, Gigi; how is my daughter doing?"

I smile. "Good morning, papa. I'm just calling to check in on you and mama."

"We are fine; we are planning to go to Italy to visit your uncle Emilio and his family and maybe spend a week in Spain; what have you been up to?"

The next hour, I discuss my job, friends, and dating life. My father and mother have always made sure we have open communication, and in doing so, I always feel comfortable talking to them about everything. It didn't always used to be this way; when I was 6, I had an older brother Fabiano 20 years older.

My father was married before my mother, and my brother was his child from his first marriage. My father worked hard and barely had time for us, and my mother was busy with her socialite duties, so by the time they realized they were too busy, my brother had taken his life. After that, my father reduced his hours, my mom pulled back from her duties, and we spent time in family counseling. I like to think what kind of man he would have been if my parents had slowed down earlier, and he got the needed support. I say goodbye to my father and grab a packed lunch and head down to my car to get to work.

Luca

"Jay, has Seamus come in yet?"

Jaime hands me the files I needed to review. "No, he hasn't, but I can guarantee he will be late." I sigh and rub my temples. I love my brother, but the man runs late when I need him.

Jaime goes behind my chair and gives me a shoulder massage, "you need to loosen up, or you are going to send yourself into an early grave". She leans down and kisses my neck. I look up to ensure my office door is closed, and I turn my chair to grab Jaime by the waist and sit her in my lap, and she straddles me. "Can I help you, sir?" I tease and keep my hands on her waist and kiss her, and she kisses me back; a bulge grows in my pants, and she grinds against it. She is wearing a pencil skirt with a short slit up the side and a light blue button-up shirt. I undo the top buttons and see she is wearing the black lacy bra I love. I undo more buttons until I can pull her right breast out of her bra, and I put it in my mouth, running my tongue around her nipples. She leans back and lets out a moan. "Luca, if you keep this up, we are going to end up fucking in your office."

I shrug. "The door is closed," a buzz sounds, and I realize it's my phone, and I groan. "Raincheck?"

I look at Jaime as she fixes herself. "Definitely." I checked my phone and saw it's Seamus showing he just arrived in the parking lot. Getting up, I put on my suit jacket and head down to warn him about being late.

After some stern stares, Seamus tells me about a car accident and traffic he dealt with. We agreed for him to buy me lunch for a week, to call it even, and we headed back to the office. The rest of the day goes by rather quickly. I have a few meetings with the board to discuss the company's performance this quarter. We are having a downturn, and I noticed morale has been depleting and wanted to talk with them. Seamus and Jaime were honest that I have been an ass lately, which may contribute to the current morale, and I started feeling bad. This team has been with me from the beginning, and we wouldn't have grown as fast as we have without them, but I have a lot on my shoulders. Our board is constantly on my ass about the company's performance, not to mention my father, who helped invest in the company, and sits on the board and sees our numbers. When I came to my father about opening a holding company right out of business school, he worried I was taking on too much and wanted me to work in corporate America for a few years and then open. I convinced him I was more than ready to open this company; with my team's determination, we grew fast, and my dad was proud and bragged to me with his colleagues and friends. After the board meeting, my dad told me that every company goes through a downturn and that I shouldn't beat myself up. I always want to make him proud because he and my mom saved me when I was young.

My parents adopted me from Ireland when I was 7; that was my happiest day. My biological mother had worked on the janitorial staff in their company's building. I don't remember much about her, but I remember she was a mean drunk who would fight with my biological father when they had one too many. I would hear them argue for hours until the neighbors called the police or when one of them left. The day my parents came to get me was when the cops showed up at my house to arrest my biological parents. They were short on money and thought it was a good idea to rob a gas station. Things got out of hand, and they killed 2 employees before taking off with all the cash in the machine. The police had asked my mother if anyone could come and get me, and since both of my grandparents distanced themselves from my parents, she gave them Ian and Marie Gallagher's names. I knew them well because I would stay with them when my mother worked overnights; they had seen me one night when my mom left me in an empty room while she cleaned and offered to watch me free. When they came to the police station, they picked me up, and I stayed with them for 2 weeks before they filed for adoption. My biological parents got handed 2 30-year sentences to run consecutively. We stayed in Ireland for another year until a business opportunity opened in Canada, and we moved.

I ended up having my staff meeting, and I thanked everyone for their hard work and gave everyone a bonus to show my appreciation and talk about this quarter's goals. After the meeting, we convinced Seamus to come out with us and celebrate the start of the weekend at McMenamins.

When we see Seamus head for his office, I wrap an arm around Jaime's shoulder and whisper, "we still have a raincheck on earlier."

Jaime giggles "after drinks, we go back to my place" I kiss her neck and reply, "that's a plan."

Jaime

I am jamming out to Shakira as I pull my Honda into my parking spot in my condo building. Once the song ends, I head to the elevator and punch my code into my condo. I am lucky I can afford the rent because Luca and Seamus pay me well for a secretary. I met them in high school, and we have been inseparable ever since; they didn't judge me for being on scholarship at our private school; they treated me all the same. Once inside my condo, I set my belongings down and hear my phone ring; looking at it, I see it's a FaceTime from my dad, and I pick it up. "Hi daddy how are you?"

He seems to look better than when I spoke to him last. I see a few more gray hairs on his beard.

"Not good; my supervisor didn't pay me enough to cover my bills. Do you think you can help me?" I sigh. Unfortunately, the authorities deported my dad back to Spain when I was in middle school. He had made a mistake and started selling drugs to bring more money into the household. My mother had no clue what he was doing; he was working as a foreman for a construction company and told mother he got a raise. When the DEA showed up at our door one night, everything came out. They revoked my father's green card after his conviction. He took a plea that allowed him to avoid serious jail time if he agreed to voluntary deportation. My mother was so angry she filed for divorce. My dad attempted to reconcile with my mother, but she was so mad, and my dad saw she wasn't budging, and he signed the papers before he left.

"yes, dad, I can send the money tonight. I will catch up with you later. I love you."

Gathering my breath, I head to my room to get ready. With my hair curled and cascading down my shoulders, I slipped into a short blue backless dress. After applying makeup to enhance my blue eyes, I examine myself in the mirror to ensure everything looks right. I am 5'3, with fair skin, blue eyes, blond hair, and a thin, athletic build, thanks to my years of soccer. My mother always told me I could stand gaining a few pounds because of how skinny I was. In school,

I used to be self-cautious about my body because I was a late bloomer while all the girls were growing. When I finally hit puberty, I had a small chest and barely there hips. Shortly after, I began playing soccer, gradually filling out but still small. I was often jealous of the other girls for having bigger chests or curves. I often thought when I got older, I would get plastic surgery. Luca and Seamus said I was fine the way I was, but my mother would make little remarks about how she had bigger chests or hips when she was my age. When I graduated from high school, I began working on my confidence and my body image issue. My mother thought I was being overdramatic and said I didn't have a body image issue because I was thin and blond. It took a few years to accept my body eventually, and once I accepted it, I had to ask myself if I wanted plastic surgery because I wanted it or because everyone else was getting it. My consensus was that I only wanted it because of what my mother was saying and that I wanted to have a bigger chest and hips because of what I saw on social media.

My mother is both my biggest fan and my toughest critic. Turning away from the mirror, I pick out my blue block heels, and as I sit on my bed, I hear the elevator open. Luca and Seamus are the only two with the codes to my condo, so it must be one or the other. I see Luca standing in my doorframe when I finish buckling my heels.

I stand, and Luca lets out a low whistle "you look good enough to eat"

I look him up and down and see that he wore a black button-up, jeans, and dress shoes. "You clean up nice," I joke, and he reaches out, grabs me by my waist, and pulls me to him. Luca moves his hand down and holds my butt, and I wrap my arms around his neck and pull him down to me to kiss him. He pushes me back against the doorframe, deepens the kiss, moves his hands behind my knee, and lifts my leg. I can feel him getting hard, and I break the kiss. "If you keep this up, we won't be going out tonight, and Seamus will get suspicious." He huffs.

"I think we should just tell Shay we have been seeing each other. It will eliminate us having to sneak around behind his back." He's been pushing to tell Shay, but I have stopped him because if we don't work out, I don't want to make Shay feel he will have to pick sides. I've known Luca since high school, and I know he won't get petty if things don't work out, but I don't want any awkwardness between the group.

"I hear you and understand why you want to tell him, but if we don't work out, I don't want things to get awkward between us, and I know you say we will work out. However, we had already broken up after our threesome experiment went sour."

Luca visibly cringes, "which was a miscalculation. Still, I did like having a third with us," he leans in to nibble at my ear.

"I did too, but if we do it again, we must make sure we choose the right person." He nods, and we hear the elevator open; we break apart, and I hurry to the mirror to make sure my makeup is in place, and Luca readjusts himself.

Seamus walks into my kitchen, and we take shots before we head out to McMenamins. I follow Seamus and Luca as we moved to an empty table in the corner of the packed lounge, where we sat down and a waiter came over to take our drink orders. Seamus and Luca order Guinness, and I order a honeysuckle cider and scan the room to see if I recognize anyone. The lounge is more packed than usual, but the vibe is energetic; a few men pass our table and stop to check me out. Luca gives them a stern look, and they continue walking. I noticed someone caught Seamus's eye.

Seamus leans over and shouts over the music, "remember the girl that hit me this morning? The one I gave my number to, she's over there with a friend."

Luca and I follow Seamus's line of sight and see a black woman with curly hair and the back of another woman's head. From what I can tell in this light, she has dark brown or light brown curly hair.

Luca nudges Seamus. "We should head over there and introduce ourselves."

Seamus shrugs his shoulders. "I don't want to seem like I am stalking the woman."

I roll my eyes. "Oh, come on, she won't think you are stalking her; it's weirder if you stand here and don't say anything. I can guarantee you she probably saw you coming in." Just as I say that, her friend turns around and makes eye contact and I get a better look at her face, and I get stunned. Her complexion is golden, with a sprinkling of freckles and light-colored eyes. She has on a dress that hugs her body and shows off her curves.

She turns her head back around, and the woman looks up and makes eye contact with Seamus, and he smiles. "We are definitely going over there." I hop down from my seat, and Seamus leads us through the crowd to her table.

We arrive at her table, and we do introductions. I found out the mystery woman is Aniyah, and her friend is Gianna. Seamus sits by Aniyah while Luca, and I sit to the left of Gianna.

I turn to Gianna. "I like your dress; it looks good on you" Gianna blushes, and I tread carefully to gauge her response to see if she is receptive to my flirting.

She looks at me and bites her lip. "Both you and Luca look good, too. I am glad Seamus brought friends with him."

I feel Luca's hand on my thigh, and he squeezes and chimes in, "well, your partner is lucky they snagged you."

She looks at the both of us. "Who said I was in a relationship? I am single; how about you two?" She takes a sip of her drink, and I take a sip of mine.

"Jaime and I are together, but we like to share with the right person."

Gianna put her drink on the table and shifted slightly. "I have never shared, but there's always a first for everything."

The atmosphere between us becomes charged, and I lean in. "We can make your first a very memorable experience if you allow us."

Her breathing hitches, and she leans in as well. "I'll be willing to try, but I have to warn you, most people get hooked after a night with me." Without thinking, I kiss her, and she kisses me back with a sense of urgency, and the noise of our surroundings melts away. I feel Luca shift, and I end up in his lap, and Gianna's hands run along my side, and she cups my left breast while I have my fingers in her hair. Luca grows hard, and his hands rub my exposed thigh.

We got lost in what we were doing and forgot that Aniyah and Seamus were sitting across from us. Seamus coughs, and Gianna and I break apart and readjust ourselves. I meet Seamus's eyes and his brows arch.

I look back at him and shrug my shoulders, and Gianna gets up and whispers in Aniyah's ear, and after some back and forth, she returns. "So, are we going to continue our night somewhere quieter?"

I smirk. "My condo is closer than Luca's; we can go back to my place."

She gets up and grabs my hand. "Let's go."

Luca and I followed her out and made the short walk back to my condo. We take 10 minutes to walk back to my building, and we take the private elevator to my condo; as soon as we step in, Gianna grabs my waist and leans down to kiss me. I didn't realize Gianna was 6 inches taller, and her heels probably added another two; I kiss her back, and Luca leads us to the couch. Gianna sits down. I straddle her, and my dress hikes further, exposing my butt. Gianna moves her hand and grabs my butt, bringing me closer to her, and I feel my buckle being released on my heel and assume Luca is removing my shoes. Once my shoes are off, he does the same with Gianna, and I break the kiss and stand to take off my dress, and Gianna follows. Once our dresses were off, Luca removed his clothes and sat on the couch in his boxers. I sit on the couch with my back to Luca's chest, my legs spread on each side of his thighs, and Gianna lowers herself to her knees.

I paused. "Hold on before we proceed. When was the last time you had a STD screening Gianna?"

Gianna replies, "I tested a week ago and I haven't been intimate since."

We pause for a minute, and Gianna and I fetch our phones from our purses, and Luca grabs his phone from his pants pockets. We pass around our phones with our mycharts pulled up and look at the results; once satisfied, we return to the couch in the same position.

"Do you want to use a condom?"

Gianna looks up at me, "no, unless you guys want to use one, I am on birth control"

"so am I, and I don't mind not using one."

I look back at Luca who shrugs "I am fine without one" once that is out of the way, Gianna takes Luca's dick out of his boxers, wraps her mouth around it, and starts sucking. Luca groans, moves his hand down my front, pulls my thong to the side, puts his finger in me, and starts moving. Luca sticks another finger in, and I grow wetter and moan as Luca brings me closer to the edge. I feel Gianna's tongue on my clit, and I look down and see Luca remove his fingers to allow Gianna entrance. Gianna eats me out, and she hits a spot that makes me moan louder, throwing my head back, and Luca leans down to kiss my neck. I feel Gianna wrap her hands around Lucas's cock and moves up and down, and it doesn't take long before we both cum.

Gianna

We head to Jaime's room, and Luca goes in first to clean up, and then Jaime goes in once he comes out. Luca has since removed his boxers, and Jaime and I also removed our thongs. While Jaime is in the bathroom, Luca comes closer to me, and I notice Luca is 2 inches taller than me and he grabs me and pulls me into a kiss. His hand rests on my lower back, and I feel him getting harder again, and he walks me back to the bed, and we lie down. Luca moves his hands over my body and parts my legs, and I am already wet from earlier actions. He guides his cock into me and pushes all the way in me, and I feel full. He moves and hits a sensitive spot. I hear the bathroom door open, and I think the bed dips slightly and look to see Jaime's mouth around my right breast. I feel her tongue circle my nipples and moan louder, and between Jaime's mouth and Luca's cock, I am overstimulated. It doesn't take long before I am cumming and panting, and we shift positions. I am lying on my back; Jaime is between my legs and has her back arched, and Luca enters her. As Luca is fucking Jaime, she eats me out and has one hand playing with my breasts. Jaime pinches my nipple, and I moan and arch my back off the bed. I move my hands through Jaime's hair and hold her hair as she eats me out. I orgasm first, then Jaime and then Luca; Jaime lays her head on my stomach, and Luca gets up.

I hear water running, and Jaime draws circles on my stomach once we have caught our breath. "So, how was your first threesome experience?"

Our eyes meet as I look down at Jaime. "I would say it was a memorable experience and hope there is a repeat in the future."

Jaime smiles "I can see another threesome in the future."

We heard the water turn off, and Luca stood at the bathroom door. "Would you ladies like to join me in the tub?"

We got up from the bed and headed to the bathroom. Jaime's tub is a decent size, and Luca gets in first, then Jaime and me; the water is nice and warm.

The bathroom is silent as we sit in the tub, and Luca breaks the silence, "so Gianna, tell us about yourself."

"I prefer to go by Gigi. My last name, Guzzo. I am 28 years old, born and raised in the beautiful city of Temecula, CA. My dad was a lawyer, and he grew up in New York, and my mother is from Cameroon. They met when she was modeling in Milan, and he was visiting family. Once they were married, my dad petitioned for my mother to come to the US. I have known Aniyah for over 4 years; we met at our call center job in Federal Way, and I live with two other roommates I've known since high school and can't think of anything else."

Jaime responds next "did you attend college, and do you plan on working at the call center in the future?"

"I didn't attend college school wasn't for me, and I bounced around from job to job until I landed the call center job. My parents help support me by paying my rent, and honestly, no, I don't want to work at the call center." The room gets quiet again. I am weary of telling them I have plans to be a stay-at-home mom due to people's judgment, and I don't know if this will even turn into a relationship.

"What do you want to do?" I leaned back on Jaime's chest.

"If I tell you what I really want to do, you might judge me."

Luca reaches his hand around Jaime's and rubs my arm. "We are the least judgmental people, so tell us."

I take a deep breath. "I don't want to work; I want to get married and be a stay-at-home mom. I want to dedicate my time to raising kids and supporting a household in the future. I might want to open a daycare when my future kid's get older."

The room gets silent again. "School isn't for everyone, and working for someone else isn't for everyone either. If Luca and I work out, we talk about kids, but we both have ambitious goals. Kids may not fit into our plans."

I turn around and sit on my knees. "What do you mean by if you don't think you guys will stay together?" Jaime and Luca exchange a look I can't decipher.

Luca responds, "we have known each other since high school. There are moments where we get along, but sometimes we are the same and butt heads." The water gets cold, and we get up, grab towels and head to the room. Jaime passes me some shorts and a T-shirt, and Luca goes to a drawer to pull out what seems to be his clothes, and Jaime dresses in a T-shirt and sweats. We head to the living room; Jaime turns on the heat and sits on the couch to continue the conversation.

Luca

I am in Jaime's kitchen warming up water and putting apple cider powder in three mugs. This night was unanticipated, but the moment I saw Gianna, it was an immediate attraction and I could tell Jaime felt it too by the way she was flirting. After the last threesome experience where the woman attempted to split Jaime and me, we agreed on not doing threesomes until we found the right person. We broke our rule tonight, but I can't help but feel Gianna is different; she worked, and we didn't have to say much, and we knew what to do like she was a missing piece. The kettle dings, and I pour the water into the three mugs, place them on the tray and head back to the living room. I set the tray on the end table and pulled out an armchair. I grab my mug, and the girls hold theirs; we sit silently for a moment, and I place my cup back on the end table to get a conversation going.

"So, we know a little about you; how about we tell you a little about ourselves? As you know, I'm Luca. I'm originally from Ireland. Seamus' parents adopted me at 7 and am 2 years older than Seamus, making me 38. We immigrated to Canada when I was 8 and then to Seattle when I was 16. I majored in finance at UCLA and attended business school there. I own my business and live on the waterfront of Point Ruston over by the movie theater."

Gianna nods and Jaime sets her cup down. "And I am from Seattle, but I was born in Barcelona, Spain, and my parents immigrated here when I was a year old. I am 35 and have an associate degree in applied science from TCC. I am finishing my business degree with a focus on accounting from UW Tacoma and working for Seamus and Luca. We all met in high school; we attended the same private school in Seattle and have been friends ever since."

Gianna also sets her mug on the table. "When did you two decide to be more than friends?"

Jaime and I look at each other. "We were on a business trip in Mexico a year ago. We had 1 too many drinks at the bar and ended up in bed together. In the morning, we had a talk and discovered we both had the same feelings for each other, and we had sex again that morning, and it was even better. Once we returned home, we agreed to try it, and we have been going strong ever since; there was one time we broke up for a short period but got back together."

Gianna picks her cup back up and drinks more, and once she is done, she sets the cup back down. "What caused y'all to break up?"

I drink the rest and put it back on the end table. "Jaime and I broke up because we had a threesome go wrong. The other woman only wanted to be with me and afterward did all she could to break us up. Her efforts led to a misunderstanding which caused an argument, and we broke up for a month. Once we both cooled down, we had a conversation and realized she orchestrated our breakup, and we both blocked her and moved on."

"So, if y'all had a bad time with the last threesome, then why did y'all decide to take me home and try again?" I like she is inquisitive and wants to know more.

"I can't speak for Luca, but you gave off good energy, and you were too beautiful to not try to bring home."

I raise an eyebrow at Jaime. "I guess you and I were thinking the same things."

Gianna looks at us, "so what does this mean for us? Will this be a onetime thing, or will we try a throuple relationship?"

Jaime and I never thought of having a polyamorous relationship; we have always thought we were monogamous and alike, which causes us to butt heads. Maybe adding Gianna to the relationship will balance us out. I can't deny that I enjoy having Gianna in our bed, but it feels like there is something there, and if Jaime is willing, I want to explore that with her.

Jaime adds, "the sex was amazing, and you attracted both Luca and me, and there's an energy between the three of us I will explore if you two want to."

Gianna and I both decide to try it, and I check the time to see it's 2am, and I see Gianna typing on her phone to who I presume is Aniyah. We carry our mugs into the kitchen, put them in the dishwasher, and return to Jaime's room. Luckily Jaime loves having space, so her bed fits all three of us just fine, and I cut off the desk lamp, and we turn it in for the night.

Jaime

The light shines through my blinds, and I roll over to find the bed empty; sitting up, I smell cinnamon rolls and bacon and head to the kitchen. I see Gianna and Luca working in the kitchen to get breakfast ready. I stand quietly for a few more minutes as they move in almost perfect harmony. For a minute, I think of what a future with the three of us can look like, the two of them cooking and I waking up our kids.

Gianna turns and sees me. "Good morning, sleepyhead. Luca mentioned he was an excellent cook, so I wanted to see for myself. Breakfast should be ready in a moment. Do you mind setting the table?"

Luca turns around and sees me, and smiles. Looking at the two of them, it's almost jarring to see how much taller they are than me. "

I can set the table." I move around the two giants and grab plates and silverware. As I set the table, Gianna and Luca brought the food and put it in the middle of my wide dining room table, and we grabbed breakfast. Eating and talking feels almost domesticated, like we have been doing this for years. We clean up the kitchen, and Luca offers to drop Gianna off at her apartment so I can get some schoolwork done. Luca and Gianna give me a light peck as they take the elevator to Luca's car.

I pull out my laptop and start working on assignments to get ahead of the class. I was working in my condo's small office when I heard my elevator door open. Assuming it's Luca, I yell I am in the office.

Luca walks through the door, still dressed in the outfit from this morning. "So, Seamus also had a good night with Aniyah. Do you want to go over there and bug him?"

I look up from typing, "what kind of question is that? Of course, I want to bug him"

Luca sends a text in the group chat asking if we can come over with food. Seamus responds we can come over and that he will just hop in the shower. We go to our favorite restaurant, which takes a few minutes, and head to Seamus' condo in the city. Seamus opens the door when we knock, and we set the table for dinner. Before Seamus moved to Point Ruston, we always came here to have dinner or game nights. When he lived in the city, we all stayed within 15 minutes of each other, and when Seamus's place wasn't available, we used mine or Luca's condo. Dinner went by smoother than I thought. Seamus told us about his night, Luca and I came clean, about our relationship and experience with Gianna, and Seamus took it well. A weight lifts from my chest, knowing we aren't hiding any secrets from him anymore and can date openly. We may have to keep it a secret in the office to prevent the rumor mill from turning and any distractions. Once dinner was over, I went to Luca's condo; since dating a year ago, we started keeping clothes at each other's places. We arrive at Luca's condo and decide to catch up on Bad Batch before the new season. At some point, I fall asleep and feel myself being lifted and taken to Luca's bed with my eyes closed. I think of what life would be like if the three of us were to work out long-term. Luca is pushing 40, and he has never been the one to settle down, and neither have I, but with me being in my mid-30s, I can't help but feel like a clock is ticking.

The rest of the weekend flies by, and on Sunday evening, I return to my place, do some cleaning, and catch up with my mother. During the conversation with my mother, I bring up my father, and she sighs. My mother still loves my father, but when he sold drugs and jeopardize my and my mother's life and status, she had no choice but to divorce him. When I talked to my mother about the divorce years later, she said that it wasn't the fact that he was selling drugs; it was the fact that he felt like there was no other option and didn't communicate with her. My mother and father have been together since they were in high school, and during that time, my father never kept secrets; she said she felt like they were a team. So, when he decided without consulting her, knowing that those actions could severely impact the family, she couldn't trust him anymore. Once the trust was gone, she couldn't continue the relationship and filed for divorce and convinced him to sign the papers. My mother applied for naturalization for her and me after divorcing, and we became naturalized after a lengthy process. By the time the call ended, I had convinced my mom to at least call my father and check in on him through the years; they have remained in contact because of me, and after I turned 18, they kept in touch.

A small part of me hopes they will reconcile, but I don't know if that will ever happen.

On Monday morning, I am awoken by a knocking on the door; looking at my alarm, I see it's 7am, and curious, I get up and head to the door. Looking out of the peephole, I see Gianna standing in the hallway with a paper bag. I open the door, and she comes charging in with a smile. I check her out, and her curly hair is in one braid to the side; she has on a blue sweater and black slacks with matching blue heels.

She looks outstanding, and I wonder if we can do a quickie before work. "Good morning, sleepyhead, I brought pastries." She beams and holds out a bag, and I close the door and head in her direction. She is already in the kitchen, grabbing plates and making coffee. I note she is a morning person, just like Luca and Seamus. I sit at the table and open the bag as she brings the plate.

I grab a blueberry muffin, and she heads back, holds 2 mugs, and returns to the table. "So, what did I do to earn a muffin and you making coffee this morning?"

Gianna finishes chewing. "Well, I was up and thought I could have breakfast with my girlfriend before work." I look at her and smile. I used to think anyone other than Luca calling me a girlfriend would sound weird, but hearing it from her lips, butterflies formed in my stomach. "It is okay to call you my girlfriend, right?"

I have a big smile on my face. "Well, what else would you call me? I am your girlfriend." I lean over, and she meets me halfway. I kiss her, tasting coffee and an apple strudel on her breath.

We break the kiss and talk while finishing breakfast. I excuse myself to take a shower and get ready for work. Once I am done, I dry off and walk into my room, naked, to find Gianna sitting on my bed.

Gianna looked over my naked body and down at the time on her phone. "It's only 8 am, and I have an hour before I need to go to work."

I smile, understanding the implication. I walk to her and straddle her lap and kiss her. She places her hands on my ass, kisses me back, and grabs me; wetness forms between my legs, and she stands and strips, not wanting to get her clothes messed up before work. She lays back on the bed, and I trail kisses down from her neck to her mound and part her thighs. I kiss the inside of her thighs, I make my way to her pussy, and I feast on her as if she was one of my last meals. She moans and orgasms on my tongue, and then she returns the favor once we are done; we get dressed and head down to the garage for work. I take 45 minutes to arrive at the office, and even with the traffic, I am still there before mostly everyone.

I turn on the lights in the office, prepare the office coffee, sort the mail, and drop it off in Seamus's office. While I am a secretary for Seamus and Luca, I also have expertise in other areas that come in handy for them. After graduating high school Luca and Seamus both went away for school and because of a lack of scholarships and money, I got a paralegal certificate from UW. I worked part-time and used the small inheritance I got from my late grandparents to pay for it. When I finished, I worked for a law firm and was making a decent salary, and when Luca opened his company, he asked me to come and work for him. I made him go through the normal hiring process he gave everyone else so I could earn my job and not have it handed to me. While dropping paperwork and mail in Luca's office, someone wraps their arms around my waist.

Luca's scent envelopes me, and I lean my head back on his chest, and he dips low and kisses my neck. "We are in the office, Luca, and the door is open."

Luca rocks me in his arms. "It's 9:30; most people don't come in until 10am" he kisses me again. I turn around in his arms and bring his mouth down to mine, and he moves his hand lower and grabs my ass. I wore my black slacks, a pink cashmere sweater, and matching heels, and he picked me up, wrapped my legs around him, walked us back, and sat me on his desk. Things started getting heavy until we heard the elevator. We break apart and straighten our clothes. I grab my paperwork and head to my desk.

One by one, the staff walks in and greets me as they walk by. Hillary attempts to greet me, but I always get the vibe she doesn't like me. It may have to do with Luca and Seamus turning down her advances and thinking I am the reason, which is not entirely wrong. Luca and I agreed to keep our relationship separate from work, and Seamus told me that Hillary was persistent after turning her down multiple times. He went on one date with her and told us it was one of the worst dates he's been on. I hear my phone ding and see they have added me to a group chat with Luca and Gianna.

Gigi: I had a good morning >. <

Luca: What did I miss?

Me: An excellent wake-up call, lol

Luca: Why wasn't I invited?

Gigi: You were, but you says, and I quote, "I am not getting up; it's too early."

Luca: Well, if I would've known what the morning would entail, I would've woken up.

Me: If y'all are down, we can have dinner at Luca's

Luca: How did my place get offered as a dinner location?

Gigi: Because I haven't been to your place, I have roommates, and we already stayed at Jaime's.

Luca: Y'all can stay if Jaime agrees to cook dinner; we cooked breakfast this weekend.

Me: Deal, I'll drop the address, and we'll meet after work

Luca: Fine by me

Gigi: Fine by me, too. Have a good day!

The rest of the day seemed to fly by, and I was in a good mood. The only thing that annoyed me was Hillary and her cronies sending me up and down to the records room to fetch paperwork. The past few months I feel as though Hillary has gotten mean suddenly. I mean, she was always snarky to me in the past, but she's never been mean. No matter how much we dislike each other, she has always been cordial to me. I even helped her coordinate the employees' community service event at the local homeless shelter she works at on the weekends. I have attempted to remain out of her line of sight for the rest of the day. Once the day is over, we head to the parking lot and see Seamus, Luca, and I are the only cars left in the parking lot. Luca got in his car, and Seamus pulled up on the other side of my car, and they waited until I started my car to leave. I try to turn over my car, and it doesn't start. I pop my hood and get out. I am parked under the parking lot light, and Luca and Seamus roll up their sleeves, and Seamus points out there is liquid in my car battery. "Why would liquid be in my car battery?"

Luca looks to Seamus "well, I think you pissed someone off, and they sabotaged your car."

I look over at Luca, who elbows Seamus. "What? That would be the only reason liquid would be in your car battery. It was working this morning, and now it's not tonight I call sabotage."

"Well, whatever happened, it's not going to get solved tonight; how about we leave the car here, and I will call a tow, and Jaime can ride with me since we are going back to my place, anyway?"

Seamus raises an eyebrow at Luca "oooh, y'all are spending the night at each other place during a workweek."

I roll my eyes and nudge him, "you are so immature" Seamus hugs us and heads out, and I grab what I need from my car and lock it up, and Luca takes us back to his place.

Gianna

I pull into the garage of Luca's building, parking in his visitor's spot, and wait for Luca and Jaime. Today was chaotic; Aniyah's ass of an ex left flowers on her desk at work. The nerve of that arrogant prick to think he can waltz back into her life after he ran off with her ex-best friend. I am in the car texting Aniyah, telling her I am spending the night with Luca and Jaime and asking her to speak later. I sent the text as Luca's car pulled into his spot as Luca and Jaime exited. I could've sworn Jaime drove her car to work this morning. I leave my car, grab my overnight bag from my trunk, and walk over to them.

I kiss them both, and we walk to the elevator. "I could've sworn you drove your car this morning; what happened?"

Jaime looks pissed and looks to Luca. "There was liquid in her car battery, causing it to die, and she had to ride with me."

The elevator opens to his condo, and we walk in. "Liquid. How did liquid get into your car battery?"

Jaime has taken off her shoes and is in the kitchen getting items together. "I know that's what I am wondering. I think someone sabotaged me, and I have a guess who did it."

I am sitting on the couch, taking off my shoes. "Who do you think it is?"

I look up and see Luca in the kitchen helping. "She probably is thinking of this woman at work; her name is Hillary, and Jaime believes she has been acting meaner lately."

Jaime is chopping vegetables. "She doesn't like me because she thinks I'm the reason for the rejections."

I get up and head to the kitchen to assist as well. I wrapped my arms around Jaime from behind and she leaned back against me. "Jealous women do crazy things."

She turns around in my arms. "Exactly! I want to bet she or one of her cronies did it, and what she doesn't know is we have cameras, and once we catch her, she gets fired."

Luca is prepping the chicken "if it was her, which it would be stupid of her to try, we would fire her."

she continues chopping, "that's all I ask." We cooked chicken fajitas, rice, refried beans, and tortillas and ate dinner. Afterwards, we cleanup for the night, and Luca turns on You and sits down to watch.

During the show, Luca is sleeping, and Jaime looks down at her phone worriedly. "Problem?"

She looks at me. "It's my father; something is going on in Spain, and he isn't being forthright about what's happening."

"Oh, your dad went back to Spain; when did that happen?" She heaves a sigh.

"He didn't go back willingly." She then explains her dad's deportation story and her parent's divorce. She tells me how she supports her father because her mother distanced herself and how she worries about him. Hearing her open up about her life, I feel guilty for not telling her and Luca about my brother. I don't speak about my brother often. The only times I've done so are with Aniyah and my roommates.

I feel guilty for not talking about him because I always get sad thinking of what he could've been. I was so young when my brother committed suicide, but I remember who he was and our time together. When I was younger, I faked not remembering him because I once brought his picture to my mom and asked about him, and she broke down. Since then, I haven't brought him up; my parents have hidden his photos, and he has become a ghost of the past.

Jaime looks at me. "Hey, I'm okay. You don't need to feel sorry for me; I've grown to learn how to cope."

I look at her. "It's not that; when I told you about myself, I wasn't candid. I had an older brother I was close to when I was younger; he was 14 years older than me. My dad was a workaholic, and my mother was a socialite who ignored my brother and me. My brother and I got closer, and he struggled with his mental health. When I was 6, he committed suicide, and I found him. I noticed that water was coming from under his door, and I opened it and found him in the tub. My parents came when I screamed, and then we were in family therapy, and my parents started working less to spend more time with me. I pretend I don't remember my brother because my parents feel guilty. They get upset," when I look up into Jaime's eyes, she has tears in them like I am, and she brings me in for a hug, and we cry together for a few moments.

Luca wakes up "uhh, what did I miss," we stop crying to giggle. "Seriously, y'all were just crying now you are laughing; what did I miss?"

We continue chuckling, and Jaime responds, "we had a girlfriend bonding moment; should've been up to be a part of it."

I nudge Jaime. "You're so mean, we can clue you in on what you missed." We talk to Luca, and he gets in the middle of us and cuddles both of us; we check the clock and see it's nearly midnight, and we decide to go to bed.

I am awoken by moaning, and I open my eyes to see Luca between Jaime's legs and her back arched. Jaime opens her eyes, sees I'm awake, and beckons me to her. I get on my hands and knees and crawl, and she kisses me while rubbing her hands on my backside.

She moans in my mouth, and I hear Luca "should I stop and watch the show?"

Jaime doesn't respond as she drags me to hover over her head, and with no words, I lower myself, and I feel her tongue in me and lean my head back. I feel hands on my breast and feel Luca's breath on my neck, and both Luca and Jaime work together to bring me to orgasm. I take a minute; Luca guides me between Jaime's legs and pushes me down so my ass is exposed and my back arched. Without a word, I eat Jaime out while Luca enters me from behind and pounds hard. It is hard to focus with Luca behind me, and when he finds the right spot, I moan into Jaime's pussy. I bring Jaime to orgasm first, and I follow next, and Luca is the last to finish.

Luca gets up and goes to start a bath, and I lay on Jaime's stomach, catching my breath while she runs her fingers through my curls. We hear the water shut off, get up, and go to the bathroom. Luca's bathroom is bigger than ours and designed in a white and black, minimalistic modern style. The tub and shower are behind a glass door, with the shower on one side and a spa tub on the other. When I enter his bathroom, I notice he has heated tiles and we make our way to the tub big enough to fit multiple people. Luca gets in, and then Jaime and I follow and sit in the tub for a while, not talking, just cuddling each other.

When the water gets cold, Luca gets out and turns on the shower, and we wash up, and Luca steps out and gets us towels to dry off.

We get ready for the workday. Jaime helps braid my hair back in three jumbo braids, and I help braid her hair and curl the ends. We make our way to our vehicles well, Jaime to Luca's, because of her car being tampered with. I arrive at work, go to my desk, set up, and go to Aniyah's desk to check in with her. She tells me how Seamus came over last night and comforted her, and I feel guilty for not being there for my best friend but grateful for Seamus being there for her. She tells me how her mother and sister are coming into town and how she is ready to talk about Seamus with them. I am happy for her she has found someone that, so far, is giving her what she deserves. I briefly tell her about my night before I have to head back to my desk to start my shift. The day goes by with no significant problems other than my supervisor eyeing me every chance he gets. It was worse when I was a probation employee, but after a chat with HR, he backed away slightly. Aniyah can't stand her supervisor because he never remembers her name, but honestly, I'll take him over mine. Luca and Jaime texted me on and off throughout the day, and I went back to my place tonight while Luca and Jaime were going to Jaime's. I love being around them, but I also like my space and must be by myself to recharge. As I am packing my bag, I hear footsteps, and thinking it's Aniyah,

I turn around only to be greeted by my supervisor blocking the entrance of my cubicle. "Hi, Gigi; getting ready to go home?"

I roll my eyes. "It's Gianna, and yes, I am. Can I help you with anything?"

"So, testy, I was just wondering if you would like to get drinks sometime?"

"I don't think so, and this conversation is making me uncomfortable. Do I need to go to HR again?"

His smile drops. "No need, just asking; I hope you have a good night." He walks away and I quickly pack up my stuff. On my way out the door I see him at another coworkers cubicle.

The rest of the week goes by, and I see Luca and Jaime on Wednesday and Thursday, and Luca offers to drive me to the airport on Friday night. Jaime's vehicle is still in the garage, and they suspect foul play, too, and we are now awaiting video records from that day. The system deletes the footage after a day and stores it in a cloud. Luca has to request that tape, and they said they should have it by Monday. Friday came, and Luca and Jaime drove me to work, and I left my suitcase in his car to go to the airport after work. Once the day ends, I meet Luca and Jaime, who doesn't take long because their office is in Auburn; we head to the airport, and I kiss them goodbye once we arrive. It's a 3 and a half hour flight to San Diego, and my dad is waiting for me outside the airport. On the way back to my childhood home, I updated my dad on what's been happening.

"Honey, have you thought about quitting? Your mom and I can support you until you find something new. How about working at a daycare?"

"A part of me thinks about that, but I don't want to leave just because they hired a predator. I already went to HR so they are aware and what will happen if I leave? He can go after another woman who doesn't have the security I have. He can threaten her job and take advantage of her. I have you guys so if I'm fired I have a back up plan. Once he gets fired I'll feel comfortable leaving. "

My dad has his eyes on the road but shakes his head "alright, honey, it's your call, but if he touches you, I will come to Federal Way and deal with him." I snort, but I know he is serious when my dad was younger, he was involved with the mafia. While that life is behind him I know he'll do anything to protect mom and I.

We arrive home, and my mother is waiting for us when we enter through the door in the garage. She opens her arms and holds me in a hug. I try to come home often, but the last month has been hectic, and I haven't seen her since Christmas. My mom cooked my favorite meal, Ndole with fried plantains, and we sat down and had dinner. After dinner, I checked my texts and saw that Luca and Jaime were glad that I got here safely, and they wished me well and Luca would pick me up on Sunday when I return. Aniyah also texted me back and said she hoped I enjoyed my weekend with my family and that we would catch up on Sunday.

I put my phone away and help my mother clean up the kitchen while my dad takes a call in his office. "So, tell me what has been going on, and don't feed me the stuff you gave your father about your boyfriend and girlfriend. How have you been feeling about the relationship?"

I dry my hands on the hand towel. "It's different from the men and women I have dated on Tinder. I always imagined myself with one person and never thought of myself with two people, but here I am. I am falling for both of them, but I am scared that I would get hurt if I allowed myself to fall. Luca and Jaime had known each other for years and were together before they met me; what if they decided they no longer wanted me? If it happens, it will hurt more than the other times because I feel like I am forming a deeper bond with them."

My mom dries her hand and holds me. "It scared me to get into a relationship with your father, too. There were stories of models falling for rich men and stopping at the top of their careers and the men dropping them. Those stories happened more often back then; most would return home crushed or become a comare or mistress. I look back and am glad I took that risk and got to meet the love of my life and have the most perfect daughter in the world."

I joke. "I'm your only daughter, so that is a little biased,"

She kisses the top of my forehead. "No, you are the most perfect daughter in my eyes, and I think you should take the chance." We finish cleaning and spend the night watching a movie on the couch as my dad comes from his office to join us.

Luca

It's Saturday, and Jaime and I are sitting on her couch, watching Hamilton wrapped up in a fuzzy blanket. Jamie and I have usually done this since we first started dating, but this time it feels different; something is missing. We have been with Gianna since last Sunday, but she has changed our relationship. Jaime and I butt heads because we are the same, and Gianna is the complete opposite, and somehow, she levels us out. I hope this works out because I have difficulty picturing our future without her. Before meeting her, I always thought Jaime and I would marry and have a family. Jaime and I experimented with threesomes, and after our last disaster of a threesome, we pulled back, and it's just been the two of us. Bringing Gianna into our bed was risky, but it ended well; she was just as into Jaime as me. We have texted Gianna a few times, not wanting to interrupt her time with her parents, but I can't wait to have her back with us on Sunday. I look down and see Jaime sleeping in my lap. Removing the blanket, I carry her into the bedroom and tuck her in.

My business phone rings just as I am about to join her in bed. I keep the business phone on in cases of emergencies. I pull my phone from my pajama pant pocket and see it's Hillary.

Checking the time, I see it's 9:30pm, and curious, I walk out of the bedroom and go to Jaime's office. "Luca speaking, what's wrong?"

"Oh, thank goodness this is Hillary. I was working on the cell phone technology contract, and I noticed a major error that couldn't wait" I remain silent, and she finishes, "the budget to buy the company is off by over $40,000, and I have read and re-read the contract, and I can't seem to find out why."

I let out a frustrated grunt; we can't afford another contract loss this quarter, and buying this company will bring in much-needed revenue for the small company and us. This contract is a win-win for both parties and if we mess up and lose it, our competitor will swoop in and take it from under us. I must fix this. "Where are you? I can get dressed and meet you."

"I am at my apartment in Fife. I can send you the address." I hang up, and head back to the bedroom, get dressed in a sweater and jeans, and kiss Jaime's forehead.

Jaime wakes briefly. "Why are you dressed?"

"The cell phone company contract has a major error, and I need to go to Hillary's place and help fix it."

Jaime sits up quickly. "Excuse me, you are going where?"

"To Hillary's place."

"Absolutely no, that plotting bitch is probably lying to get you in her bed."

I sigh and lean my head on the door frame; this isn't going to go well. "I have to check if we lose this contract. The company will take another hit, and it will force me to take drastic measures to keep from going under. You trust me, right?"

She stays silent with her arms folded.

"Really, Jay, you are going to play this game; this is business,"
she still is quiet.

"Well, if you are going to act like a baby, I have to get going."

She continues to give me the silent treatment, and I roll my eyes. I go to kiss her, and she turns her head.

"I'm not putting up with us. Once I'm done at Hillary's, I'm going back to my place. I will text you when I get home." I leave before she responds.

While in the car, I blast my playlist to take my mind off whatever happened earlier. Whenever she doesn't get her way, she gives me the silent treatment. We have talked about this, and she keeps saying she will try to communicate better. I hit the wheel. When Jaime's parents were still together, she told me that her mother used to pull this stunt to get her way, and I told her I didn't want that to be in our relationship and we should communicate. I arrived at Hillary's and checked my texts to see Gianna texted.

Gigi: What happened? Jaime called me crying.

Me: I had to leave to go to Hillary's handling an urgent business matter. She didn't want me to go and gave me the silent treatment.

Gigi: Hillary as in the woman at work that Jaime thinks has it out for her? Are you meeting her at her house?

Me: Yes

Gigi: Luca, use your brain. She's setting you up. y'all should meet in public.

Me: Too late. I'm already here.

Gigi: Please be careful and call me once you get home. I'll talk to Jaime.

Me: Thank you

I headed to Hillary's apartment and knocked on the door. Hillary answers in a tight shirt that plumps up her breast and form fitting yoga pants. She has her brunette hair in a messy bun on top of her head, and I can tell she has put a little makeup on, and I follow her indoors and roll my eyes. I know fully that she is interested in either Seamus or me. After Seamus went on a date with her and then decided it wouldn't work out, she set her eyes on me. I don't like her and never will, and I have told her that in a kinder way than Seamus did, but I guess she took my kindness as a, maybe.

I follow her into her apartment to her living room, sit on her couch, and see the contract on her coffee table.

She sits down a little too close to me. "You want anything to drink?" She bats her eyelashes.

"No, thank you. Can you show me the error so we can correct it?"

The smile fades, and I hope she took my tone as I am only here for business and not pleasure. We worked for over an hour, found the error, corrected it, and signed for Seamus to review tomorrow.

"I can drop the paperwork off to Seamus's condo on my way home."

She smiles. "That's so sweet, but I will be in the area and I can drop it off to him."

"Thank you. I would rather have everything be digital, but Seamus wants to keep paper files on file."

"I understand."

I reach for the door handle and Hillary trips, and I catch her and stand her up. She smiles. "Such a gentleman." She bats her eyes and steps her closer to me.

I don't like where this is going and I try to leave before she attempts to lean in and kiss me.

I give her a light shove to put distance between us. "I'm not interested in you, Hillary. This was highly inappropriate and come Monday you, me and HR will have a meeting."

"I'm sorry Luca, I thought you were."

I opened her apartment door and turn around. "Give me the paperwork and I will drop them off to Seamus."

She hands me the paperwork, and tears are forming in her eyes. "I'm sorry."

I make my way to my car; and text the IT team to suspend her access to our database. I called Seamus to get his legal advice to get ahead of this fallout.

"Yo, what's up, bro?"

"Hillary tried to kiss me when I was at her house."

"Wait, you were in Hillary's house?" I hear a TV being muted "Explain."

"I came here to fix some paperwork and when I tried to leave, she kissed me."

"Ok, so send an immediate email to HR and explain what happened. Do not talk to Hillary anymore until Monday."

"Okay, thanks." I hung up and sit in the parking lot and emailed HR about the incident.

I try to call Jaime on the way home, and she doesn't pick up, probably still mad at me, and I check the time and see it's 10:45pm. When I get home I pace around and call Gianna.

"Hi Luca, what's up?"

"You were right, Hillary tried to kiss me. I shoved her away and emailed HR."

The line is quiet before she responds. "How are you doing?"

"I'm freaking out. What if she turns this around and ruins the company? I have people relying on the company's success for their paychecks."

"Take a deep breath."

I take a deep breath.

"Okay now you did the right thing by emailing HR and this wasn't your fault. I will be back tomorrow, but for right now, take a breath and relax."

"I will try." Once I hung up the phone, I turned on the TV and let it play in the background until I got tired. I cannot sleep, worried about what will happen come Monday.

I toss and turn, and my alarm goes off at 8am to head to SeaTac to pick up Gianna, and I hear a knock at the door. Fearing Hillary called the cops and lied, I throw a shirt on and head for the door. I opened the door to find Jaime at the door with coffee and a brown paper bag, and I moved to allow her to come in.

She sets the coffee and bag on the dining room table, turns, and hugs me. I wrap my arms around her and hold her tight.

"I am so sorry last night. You did nothing wrong, and I was being petty. I trust you, but I didn't trust her. We will work through whatever comes our way."

I kiss her forehead, sit down on the dining room chair, and put my head in my hands. "I should have just told her it could wait until the morning and stayed at your place."

I feel Jaime's hands lift my head. "This isn't on you, it's on her. She should have respected your boundary." I look up at her. She bends down and kisses me. "Now let's get some food in you and get you changed so that we can pick up our girl." We have a bite, I switch my clothes, and Jaime and I drive to SeaTac.

The tense silence between us grows as we avoid discussing what happened last night before I left for Hillary's apartment, with the added frustration of an unusual amount of traffic filling the car ride to the airport. It's a familiar pattern after one of our arguments. I don't press the issue because I have learned that this is her typical behavior, and I want to avoid another argument. She knows she is immature but doesn't want to admit to it because it acknowledges that she has taken on her mother's toxic trait. I've known her for a while, so I know she loves her mother but can't tolerate her mother's relationships.

Her mom dated a few guys after the divorce, but they never lasted because of her controlling ways. Jaime hoped her parents would be together, but then she realized it wasn't meant to be. After high school, her dad dated a pleasant woman, but her mom found out and refused to answer his calls or talk to him because of his girlfriend. He broke up with his girlfriend to reestablish a relationship with her mother and have her speak to him. I look at her and see her scrolling through her phone, avoiding speaking. I want to tell her to look in the mirror and know she might ruin us if she doesn't stop the manipulation. We arrive and wait for Gianna; we see her, and she comes rushing over to us, and I go out to help with her bags.

Jaime

The car ride gets better when Gianna gets in the car and tells us about her trip and her plane ride. In the back of my mind, I replay the events of last night, and all I can think of is the intense embarrassment that lingers. I was furious when he woke me up to go to Hillary's, and I strongly opposed him going. To make him stay, I gave him the silent treatment. I trust him, but not her. My intuition was right about Hillary. The silent treatment is how my mom would manipulate my father, exes, and sometimes me when she wanted something to go her way. When I was a child, it used to bother me when my mother ignored me, so I would act out to get her attention until she would finally communicate her expectations. While my mother has good intentions, she is only doing what she learned from her mother. When she tried the tactic and it worked for her, she continued using it. I know I am doing the same thing I have always judged her for, and I'm scared to address it. Every time it happens, I keep saying that I will not do it again, and no matter how much I fight it, I do it again. Gianna told us she wanted to spend the night alone, then she gave us a peck goodbye before going to the elevator.

"You can drop me off at my place, and I will see you Monday."

Luca looks at me. "No," he responds as he drives us back to his place.

The air is stifling as we make the brief trip to Luca's condo, and the elevator ride is quiet. We arrive at his condo, and I go to his office with a reading nook to hide out until we go to bed.

Luca stops me, "we need to talk now."

"I'm tired. Can we talk about whatever we need to another time?"

"No, we need to talk tonight."

He walks over to his kitchen to pour two glasses of hard cider and makes his way to the couch. He waves to me, and I follow him, take a glass, and look down at my drink, hoping to avoid this conversation.

"Last night can't happen again," I go to interrupt him. "I am not finished; you keep saying it won't happen, yet here we are again. For years, I have kept silent about it, and especially during the past year. I keep ignoring it and allowing you to get away with it, but I can't keep going like this. I don't want you to bring it into our relationship with Gianna." He takes a sip from his drink, and I can't hold my tears back. I take a drink and compose myself before speaking.

"I am sorry, and I know I do it and try not to. I can't help it, and I know I need to learn communication skills instead of giving you the silent treatment." Tears are streaming down my face. Luca puts his glass on his coffee table, grabs mine, and puts it there too.

He pulls me into his lap. "It wouldn't hurt to go to therapy and find out why you keep doing it, and I can join you. I know I can learn some communication skills, too. It wasn't healthy for me to hold this in for so long. We can even invite Gianna and make it a couple's therapy."

I laugh a little. "Yeah, I think we all have something to work on. So, you are thinking she is going to be long term too?"

I look up at him. "Yea, I am falling for her and want both you and her in my life, and I want us to build a family."

I look him in the eyes. "I want that too; I want us to build a family with her. I don't care that she wants to be a stay-at-home mom; that job is just as hard as any 9-5."

He kisses me. "I hope she says yes."

We spent the rest of the night cuddling and talking on his couch. I assured him he won't be the one to get in trouble and that Hillary had been planning this from the moment Seamus said no. That night, Luca and I share a different kind of intimacy, as our lovemaking takes on a slow and sensual pace, unlike our usual preference for rough sex.

Luca woke up and seemed like he got more sleep last night. Gianna sends a text to the group chat.

Gigi: Everything will be fine. You did nothing wrong. Let me know what happens after the meeting.

The car ride to the office was silent, and Luca gripped the steering wheel. I can tell by his face that he is worried about the outcome of the HR meeting today. I reach out and place my hand on Luca's thigh, and he relaxes a little; we also arrive in the parking lot and see Seamus's vehicle. Seamus gets out and walks over to our car, and we get out to greet him.

Seamus brings Luca in for a hug. "I got your back, brother,"

Luca hugs him tighter. "Whatever happens today, thank you for always having my back."

We walk into the office together, and I go through the daily opening chores as employees trickle in, and as I leave the break room with a cup of coffee, I almost walk into Hillary.

"Oh, hi Jaime, you look pretty today." She smiles, walks over to her desk, and sets her stuff down.

I continue to my desk and see Luca leave his office toward the HR office, and I get a message from HR to get Hillary. I set my coffee down and walked over to Hillary's desk. "Hey Hillary, HR is requesting you to go to their office now."

She looks up, and she goes pale. "Yes, of course. I will be there in a minute. Uh Jaime, can I ask you a question?"

"Sure, what's up?"

She looks around. "I'm assuming you heard about what happened this weekend, right?"

"I have been friends with Seamus and Luca since high school; yes, I heard, and no I don't want to talk to you about it."

Her facial expression turns, and she turns her back and walks away from me towards the HR office. I return to my desk and get started on the to-do list on my desk.

I get some work done and keep myself distracted while the meeting happened. When I look up at the clock on the wall. I realize it's been 2 and a half hour since the meeting started."

I hear a door open and see Seamus leaving his office. "I'm going to grab lunch at Subway; you want anything?"

I'm getting ready to reply when we see Hillary coming around the corner with tears, heading to her desk. HR and security are walking in her direction. Luca comes to my desk, and Seamus and I remain silent until HR and security disappear around the corner.

"Luckily, she admitted to what she did and tried to beg to keep her job, and we fired her. She thought I was interested in her, and she was under a lot of stress and made a mistake."

"She knew you had no interest in her, but it's over now, and I received an email from security with the video from last week. I can forward it to you."

"Thank you, Jay, and if y'all are hungry, I was thinking of Subway for lunch."

Seamus and I laugh. "I got some more work to do, but if y'all are going, can y'all get me my normal order?"

They nod and head out to grab lunch and return to my tasks.

Gianna

Jaime texted me to let me know everything went well, and that they had fired Hillary and she left the office without incident. I smile briefly, return to the customer, and look at the time; it's 2pm and time for my lunch. As soon as I log off the phone, I get a message to meet with my supervisor; before going to lunch, I roll my eyes, lock my computer, and head to my supervisor's office.

I knock on the door, and he replies, "Come in." I step into his office and keep the door open.

"Close the door."

I look at the door. "I am not comfortable with the door being closed."

He looks up at me and huffs, "Fine, sit, please" I take a seat. "We need to have a conversation about your performance. I see that your metrics are the lowest in the unit. I think you need an additional 1 on 1 training that I can provide."

I try not to roll my eyes. "Last time we spoke, you told me I was doing fine; your words were exactly "Keep up the good work, and I can see you on a supervisor track" So what changed?"

He purses his lips. "Yes, I remember, but I reviewed your metrics again and saw some overlooked errors I had to review. I spoke to HR, and they said it was okay to train you one on one during work hours."

I fake a smile. "I understand. You can send me an email with the schedule, and I am late for lunch." Without his response, I leave his office and head to lunch. I luckily caught Aniyah at lunch, and we ate and caught up, and she said that the 1 on 1 mentoring sounded sketchy.

The rest of the day goes by as well as a Monday can go, and I am ready to leave by the time I clock out. I sent a text message to the group chat to let them know I would meet them at Luca's home after I had gone home and packed a bag. I say my goodbyes to passing coworkers and the security guard. I make it to my car and receive a notification; thinking it's a group chat, I open the message to see it's a DM on my Instagram. It's from someone I have never seen before; the message reads.

Hi; you don't know me, but I think you might be my aunt. Before I was born, my mother had an affair with your deceased brother 14 years ago. My mother assumed I was my dad's child, but the affair came to light, and we got a DNA test. The DNA test showed I wasn't my dad's child, and she was adamant that Fabiano Guzzo was the only person she had an affair with. I searched online for an obituary for your Fabiano and found that he had a sister. I am unsure if I got the right person, but I would like to speak with you if that's fine.

The message shocked me, and I clicked on her page and saw that she recently celebrated her 14th birthday in December. I see pictures of her in a cheerleader uniform, and I stare at her picture and see features of Fabiano and my father on her face. From what I remember, there were a few friends at Fabiano's funeral, and I don't remember seeing a girlfriend or lover. I continue to stalk her Instagram; if she is, in fact, my niece, then that means a piece of Fabiano is living, and I can have a relationship with her and tell her about her father. I replied I would love to speak with her, sent her my contact information, and asked to talk to her this weekend. If she's Fabiano's daughter, I'll tell my parents, but I'll wait till I get a DNA test done to make sure. My mother treated Fabiano like her son after my father's 1st wife died. My mother wasn't perfect, and she allowed her socialite duties to take priority over us. If she could go back in time, she would withdraw from some charity boards she was on and focus on us, but we can't change the past.

It takes nearly 50 minutes to get back to my apartment because of excess traffic and because of the concert at the Tacoma Dome. I pack a suitcase of clothes until Sunday, assuming I will stay with them for the rest of the week. Aniyah and I joked earlier about how much our life has changed in the last 2 weeks and how we went from single ladies hanging out every weekend to being in committed relationships hanging out with our significant others. I am glad we are dating brothers and friends because we have discussed doing group dates in the future.

I am getting ready to leave when my roommates stop me. "Hey Gigi, we need to talk to you before you leave."

I set my suitcase by the elevator and joined them in the living room. "Hey, what's up?"

My roommates looked at each other. "We wanted to talk to you about our lease. The lease ends at the end of February, and Rosie and I have been thinking about what's next."

I look between Rosie and Jessie, and Jessie speaks up, "We love being your roommate, but it might be time we all go our own way. My boyfriend is graduating, and plans on moving to Seattle, and Rosie is considering moving back to California for a new job opportunity. We will all remain friends, but I think it's time we all take the next step in our lives,"

We all have lived together for 4 years, and we've known each other since high school, and it's weird to think we won't be living together. "I guess you are right, but it's still going to be sad for all of us to not live together; Rosie, what job opportunities do you have in California?"

Rosie looks at me. "Well, you have been busy with your relationship, and I didn't know if I would get it. Hulu offered me a job as a programmer, and the money they have offered is almost triple what I am making now."

I squealed and hugged Rosie. "Congratulations, we can visit once you're settled, and Jesse, does this mean wedding bells are in the future?"

Jessie smiles. "I think he got offered a job at a law firm in Seattle and wants me to move in with him. I have already started applying for a teaching job in the Seattle school district,"

I smile. "We better be bridesmaids at your wedding."

We giggle and hug one another. "So, Jessie and I have plans; what will you do? Will you move in with Jaime and Luca?"

"I honestly don't know. I haven't thought of that, but our current relationship is nearly perfect. I think we may get married, but that is a logistics we will have to work out."

We talk for a few minutes before I head out to Luca's, and I have more on my mind with everything going on. I enter Luca's condo elevator code and see Jaime and Luca cooking in the kitchen together. Fall Out Boys is playing in the background, and I unpack my suitcase in Luca's room. When I open his closet, I see his clothes, Jaime's clothes, and I see a space, and I get emotional to know that he took the time to make space for me. Once I finish putting up my clothes, I change into a tank top and shorts and head for the kitchen.

I kiss Jaime, then Luca. "Do you guys need help with anything?"

"Can you help by setting the table? Can you also make a salad for dinner too?"

I look back at Jaime to see her checking on the lasagna. "Sure, I can help."

I move in between them to get the dishes for the table. Once I set the table, I grab a bowl, some lettuce, and other fixings, make a cranberry, feta, and walnut salad, and put it in the middle. We completed the rest of dinner, gathered around the table for the meal and shared details about our days, then tidied up afterward. Jaime grabs wine and three glasses, and we sit on the couch.

Jaime takes a sip of her wine. "Do you think we are moving too fast as a couple?"

I set my wine down. "Maybe? But we have to do what's comfortable for us. I have been thinking about our relationship. This may be fast, but I'm falling for both you and Luca, and it scares me. I keep thinking about what if you guys decide that you no longer want me and I get heartbroken?"

I sucked in a deep breath and Luca hugged me close while Jaime cuddled up to us and rubbed my thighs. "We will not leave you because I don't know how to explain it, but you fit like a missing puzzle piece, and I think I can speak for Jaime and say that we aren't going anywhere."

I look at Jaime. "I am not going anywhere, and Luca is right; you are our missing piece."

A weight lifts off my chest, and we three cuddle on the couch. "I think my brother has a daughter; she messaged me on Instagram.,"

Jaime sits up and turns to me. "Did you respond? And how old is she?"

"I did and asked to speak with her; she is 14. I was young when he died, and I don't remember hearing that my brother was seeing anyone, but I don't think he would've told anyone. According to the girl, her mother had an extramarital affair with my brother, and she thought another man was her father."

Luca rubs my arms. "I can cover the DNA testing cost. Do you hope she is your niece? How do you feel?"

"A part of me wants her to be his so we can have a piece of him still alive. My parents haven't talked about him in years and avoid the topic. Having a niece will force my parents to speak about him finally. They don't talk about him because they don't want to relive their guilt for not paying attention to us and being less-than-stellar parents. My parents weren't terrible, but their priority of giving us a lavish lifestyle overshadowed their role as parents. He had high expectations for my brother and expected him to follow in his footsteps. My brother got accepted into law school, which made my father proud, but my brother hated it."

Jaime rubs my thigh again. "I think parents think they are doing their best based on their upbringing, and I don't think they realize they have childhood trauma and think they are doing better than their parents. My mother said that her parents would yell at each other for hours, her father was an alcoholic, and her mom was overmedicating and zoned out. Her parents taught her to never talk about house business outside the house, so she and her two sisters suffered in silence. My dad's parents weren't any better, either. My dad's father had an addiction problem that he never sought help for."

Luca looks between the both of us. "When we have a family, I want us to agree to not make the same mistakes as our parents. I want us to have open and honest conversations with our kids and each other. Despite having really shitty biological parents, I consider myself lucky to have gotten the best adoptive parents someone could ask for. I wonder if maybe they had counseling and alcohol and drug intervention, what parents they would've been to me."

I look between Jaime and Luca. "We can't go back and change our parents or dwell in the past, but we can make better decisions for the future. We can get therapy when one or all of us is falling short of our promises and to share the workload so one person isn't carrying more than the next person."

I get a notification on my phone, and I lean over and pick up my phone on the coffee table and see it's an Instagram message. I saw the girl had responded and asked to speak Friday night, and I also checked the time and saw it was approaching midnight. We get up, head to Luca's bedroom, get ready for bed, and turn off the lights.

Luca

Starting on Tuesday, the number of meetings seemed endless this week. I have had an increasing number of board meetings, which is expected because of this quarter's performance, but things seem to turn around. We have secured the acquisitions of 3 more companies and created contracts that work for everyone, and word is spreading about us. Seamus's replacement has taken on more work, and I may let Seamus go sooner than I planned. Seamus has promised to stay on for another year to train his replacement, but Jasmine, the woman hired to replace him, has been remarkable. On Thursday, I got a call from my mom to ask how I had been doing, and I updated her about the past three weeks.

I feel bad that I've been so busy I haven't been calling mom as often as usual, but I have been avoiding calling her because I am unsure how she would feel about my relationship.

She is silent for a few minutes. "Luca, you already know how I feel about marriage. I don't understand your situation, but if it's making you happy, I will learn to accept it. I just want to ensure this is what you want and if this situation makes you happy."

"I am truly happy with Jaime, but something always felt missing. Until we met Gianna, we both have been in a weird space, and since she came into our lives, we feel like our relationship is complete and has improved."

"I hear you, but are you with her because she fills in a gap, or are you with her because you truly see a future with her?"

Without hesitation, I answer, "I truly see a future with her, and so does Jaime; we want to make this work. We want to get married, but I know we can't legally do it, so I was thinking about doing a commitment ceremony with the three of us and legally marrying Gianna."

"How do you think Jaime will feel about you legally marrying Gianna instead of her?"

My mom has a good point. "I was thinking about talking to Jaime about it to see what she is thinking."

"That sounds like the intelligent thing to do, and I hope you three come to a resolution that works for everyone. I also want to have you guys at the house for dinner when you guys are ready." I stay on the phone for a few more minutes and hang up to get back to work.

Friday comes, and Gianna wakes up with nervous energy. Jaime and I try to get her to eat and calm her nerves. To quell our concerns, she eats some avocado toast and drinks tea. Jaime has agreed to go with her to meet with her potential niece, and I am glad at least one of us will be there for moral support. Last night, we came to a consensus that my coming along may make the girl uncomfortable and cause her to leave without having a conversation. Jaime's car finally got repaired, and she got it back on Monday. I still haven't checked the security tape because of the Hillary situation earlier this week, but I promised Jaime I will look at it.

We all head to work, and thankfully today is the calmest it's been this week, and I open the security tape. And I see a familiar brunette with what looks like a water bottle prying Jaime's hood open and pouring the liquid into her battery. I owe Jaime an apology because she was right all along that Hillary had some vendetta against her. I press the button on my desk to buzz Jaime, and it takes less than 2 minutes for her to enter my office. "Close the door, please."

She closes the door and crosses the room. "I'm sorry you were right. Hillary is pouring liquid into your battery on the video,"

She smiles. "I know this isn't the right response, but I told you that heifer had it out for me."

She comes around my desk to look at the video. She is bent over slightly, and I lean back to check out her ass. Looking up to ensure the door is closed, I smack her ass, and she slaps my knee without looking back.

"What, I can't appreciate the view?"

She turns around and leans on the desk facing me. "You can appreciate it when we leave work."

She leans down and gives me a quick kiss before we hear a knock at the door. She straightens, grabs her documents, and heads out the doorway as finance team members come in for our afternoon meeting.

The clock strikes 5, and I am more than ready to be done with this chaotic week. I start my closing duties, and Seamus and Jaime come into my office without knocking.

"Why do you shut down right at 5? If you start it 10 minutes before, like everyone else, you can leave exactly at 5." Seamus sits on the arm of my office couch.

"Unlike your lazy tail, my work doesn't end 10 minutes before we close," Seamus sticks his tongue out at me.

"I'm surrounded by kids. Do I need to put you guys in time-out?"

I give Jaime a look. "You can put me in time-out whenever you want."

Jaime looks at me lustily.

"Get a room, you two." Seamus bemoans.

"Technically, you are in my room."

Seamus grabs his stuff. "I'm going to head out and meet Aniyah before y'all end up ripping each other clothes off."

We wave off Seamus, and Jaime looks. "Well, I need to get going if I am going to meet with Gianna in time; she set up the meeting at a boba place in Tacoma. Apparently, her niece lives in Lakewood and is getting a ride from a friend, so her mother doesn't know."

She leans down to kiss me and heads out the door.

Getting ready to leave, I get a notification that I chose not to check because I want to get out before something else tethers me here. I am glad Gianna is getting the answers she needs, and Jaime and I would have to figure out what to do with the Hillary situation. Luckily, Hillary and Gianna's family situations are the only two major issues we are dealing with, which, in hindsight, are not something too crazy to handle. I get in my car, lock the door, and look at the notification before I drive, and I see a DM on Facebook and sigh. Why does everything go down in the DM? I open the message and am not prepared for what I see; I see a picture, and as I zoom in closer, I realize it's a blond Hillary lying naked on Jaime's bed. I am glad Jaime is with Gianna because if Jaime sees this, she will catch a felony for this picture alone. Taking a deep breath, I start the car, and instead of driving home, I go to Jaime to handle the situation before it gets out of hand. I choose not to tell Jaime so she can help Gianna, and honestly, I don't know if I am doing the right thing or something idiotic.

As a precaution, I contacted the head of my private security team to meet me at Jaime's place to make sure I had a witness to this craziness.

Jaime

I arrive at the Bobalust café that Gianna recommended, spot her car, park mine next to it, and enter. I order a blended peach mango and strawberry with peach bits, add honey boba on the bottom, and locate Gianna sitting at a table in the corner.

I slid in next to her and kissed her. "How are you feeling?"

"I am absolutely nervous; what if she isn't my niece, and I am causing myself more pain by meeting with her, but if I don't, I will regret it forever?"

Just as she finishes, the bell rings. We look at the door and see a tall, medium build teenager with brownish-blonde hair tied in a pony. She has olive skin with hints of freckles on her cheek and is wearing a pink sweater, jeans, and Converse; Gianna stands and grabs her attention, and she walks in our direction and Gianna sits back down.

She sits down and smiles. "Hi, I am Nova Ricci; thank you for agreeing to meet." She holds out her hand, and we shake her hand.

"Do you want some boba on me?"

She looks at Gianna. "You don't have to do that."

"It's our treat; pick out what you want, and Jaime can get it for you."

She gives me her order, and I leave the table to give them a moment to speak. The line had gotten longer, and I looked over and saw that the conversation seemed to go well, and once I got to the register, I ordered Nova's drink. It takes a few minutes, and by the time I return to the table, they are smiling with a few tears in their eyes.

I sat down and passed the drink to Nova. "So, what did I miss?"

They laugh, and they discuss the location where to get the DNA testing done, and Nova looks at the time on her phone and informs us she has to go home. She leaves with her friend, and Gianna and I talk for a few more minutes.

Once we finish our drinks, we walk hand in hand out to our vehicles. Gianna and I lean against the driver's side door, and she kisses me while I run my fingers through her hair; We cut our kiss short when Gianna's phone rings.

She picks up the phone and listens intently, and she says nothing and hangs up. "I need to get a few things from my place. Can you follow me back?"

"Umm, sure, but who were you on the phone with?"

"Oh, that was an automated call to remind me of an appointment, but seriously, I need to go back to my place; then we can go to Luca's."

"Sure, I can follow you."

We get into our cars, and I follow Gianna into her parking garage and the elevator. Gianna goes to her bedroom, and I sit on her couch and scroll through my phone and see a notification from the front desk manager that sends me on high alert. *Hi, Ms. Cabrera; just following up; your sister came by and informed me you were expecting her. I let her up to your place. Next time, please let us know if guests need to be let up.*

I don't have any sisters. I only have 2 brothers and they are in different countries.

I yell to Gianna, "we need to get back to my place now; my dumb front desk manager let someone up to my condo!"

Gianna came around the corner with her suitcase and didn't look surprised. "Yeah, I know, I lied earlier. Luca called and told me Hillary got into your place, and he took his security to take care of it. Don't be mad at him; Luca asked me to keep you distracted so you don't end up with a felony."

I take a deep breath and think before I speak, because I am pissed. I can understand why he kept me out of it; back in our 20s, there was a bar fight because a man danced with me, and his girlfriend wasn't happy. I tried to diffuse the situation, but we fought when she threw her drink in my face. The police handcuffed me at the night's end, and the woman spent a night in the hospital. Seamus worked his magic, and I ended up with community service and anger management and served 5 months of probation.

"Okay, I understand why he asked you to keep me distracted, but she broke into my condo, and I want to face her."

She pauses and takes out her phone. "I'm going to call Luca and see what's happening."

She calls Luca, speaks with him for a moment, and then puts Luca on speakerphone.

"Jaime, I don't think it's wise for you to come over; let me handle this. The cops have been called and are currently arresting her for breaking and entering."

I pause for a beat. "Thank you, so can Gigi, and I can go to your place. I have your access code."

"Yeah, that's fine. I will meet you guys when I am done."

I helped Gianna carry her bags down to the garage, and we took my car and leave hers here this weekend. We take a few minutes to reach Luca's parking garage, and I key in the code to his condo, and the elevator ride up is quiet. Once inside, Gianna took her bag to Luca's room, and I headed to the kitchen to start dinner. I am going to cook chicken biryani and heat some Naan that Luca bought this week. In the middle of cutting up the chicken, the elevator dings, and I look around the corner to see Luca coming in, looking exhausted. I return to cooking and put the chicken, ghee, and onion in the instant pot to sauté. Dinner is almost ready; I see Luca and Gianna coming out of the bedroom, wearing casual clothes and looking slightly flushed. I can assume they got a little action before dinner. Luca and Gianna come into the kitchen, and each kiss me on the cheek, and they get the table ready.

"Dinner smells wonderful, Jay; thank you."

"You're welcome next time one of you guys is cooking."

"We should all write up a cooking schedule so that one person isn't cooking more than the next person."

I am dishing up servings in bowls. "That is a good idea, Gigi; we can work one up this weekend; now y'all come to grab your dishes."

I plated the Naan, cut it up, and placed the plate in the middle of the table. We have a Friday dinner where we talk about our days and crack jokes, and this feels right. Once dinner, we clean up, grab a bottle of wine, and turn on Hulu. Gianna turns on 9-1-1, and halfway through the episode, I get a notification and open my phone. I open my phone to see a message from my father, which reads:

Papi: Hi baby girl, I'm in big trouble. When you receive this, please call me as soon as possible.

That message grabs my attention. "Whoever has the remote, pause it for a minute,"

Luca pauses the show. "What's wrong?"

I don't respond. I call my father on FaceTime,

"Dad, what's wrong?" He looks the worst I have ever seen him.

"I got involved with some loan sharks and thought I could pay them back. They added interest and the money you sent me was used to pay them back, but now they say I owe them an extra 500 if I don't pay them in 2 hours."

I am shocked and mad at my father for making dumb decisions and expecting me to bail him out, but I don't have any other options. I don't want my father to end up dead. We are going to have a long discussion about his decisions, and I will have to put my foot down. "I can send you this money, but dad, we're going to have to talk more about your decisions. I'm your daughter, I shouldn't have to bail you out."

"Thank you, baby, I love you."

I hung up and began the money transfer as fast as possible. Luca and Gianna still look at me to figure out what's going on after the transfer is complete; I breathe and cry. Luca picks me up, sits, and places me on his lap. Gianna scoots over, leans over, puts her head on my shoulder, and wraps her arm over my lap.

"Jay, what happened?"

I look at Gianna, then Luca and I go over my father's story and what I had to do to save him. Luca and Gianna wrapped me tighter.

"I am so tired of carrying my parents on my back emotionally and financially. My mother isn't as bad as my dad, but she pulls her manipulative tactic to make me feel bad about not visiting her or getting her a better gift. They think I am swimming in cash because I have a well-paying job and a downtown condo."

Gianna wipes a tear from my face. "That shouldn't be your job to care for your parents; I'm not saying you shouldn't give your parents anything, but it should be when you want to, not when they demand."

I smile at her and respond, "you and Luca are lucky enough to come from well-off parents who don't have to worry about if your parents are okay or if they have enough money."

Luca rubs my back and says, "even though Gianna and I have affluent parents, there's more to us than meets the eye."

"We all have family issues but have each other to lean on. Maybe therapy isn't a bad idea."

Luca and I look at Gianna and laugh a little, but she has a point; maybe therapy will help us as individuals and as a couple.

We eventually move to the bedroom, brush our teeth, change into pajamas, and cuddle in Luca's bed until we fall asleep. I am awoken by a phone ringing and vibrating; looking over at the bedside table, I see it's Gianna's phone. I see

Luca waking up, too, and see Gianna is still sleeping. This woman sleeps like a rock on the weekends. I picked up her phone to see it was her potential niece calling, which is odd that the teenager is up at 4am on a Saturday morning.

I shake Gianna a few times, and she awakens. "Why are you waking me up? The sun isn't even up." She places the pillow over her face.

"Your potential niece called, and I think it's an emergency because she called 3 times."

Gianna sits back up and grabs her phone from my hand while Luca lays back down, scrolling on his phone, and Gianna dials the number back. The other line picks up on the 2nd call. "Gianna, I'm sorry I wasn't going to tell my mom about meeting with you, but she found out. I don't think we need to do the DNA test because Fabiano did a DNA test when I was born, and it was positive he was my father. I don't know if I should be happy or mad because she knew all this time and lied to my dad about the paternity."

Luca and I look at Gianna, unable to gauge her feelings, and tears form in her eyes.

"That's great news that she has the test, and I feel you. I don't know how I should feel either. I still think we need to do another paternity test to have a more recent one."

Luca rubs on her thighs, and I rub her back as the conversation continues. They stay on the phone for a few more minutes, and when they hang up, Gianna cries. We give Gianna a few minutes to cry, and Luca says, "isn't it a good thing that you know you have a niece?"

Gianna looks over at Luca. "Yes and no; all this time, I've had a niece, and my parents had a grandchild, and we have missed out on years of her growing up. I am not a mother, so I wouldn't have known what I would've done in that position. 'However, both her mother and my brother have equal parts in creating this situation".

I rub her back as she cries some more, and I can't imagine what she is going through. When I was younger, I always wished I had siblings I was close to; technically, I have 2 other siblings. My parents split briefly before marriage, and my father had 2 sons. My mother took my father back, and my father has a relationship with them. I visited them a few times when I went to Spain with my parents and then when I visited my father after his deportation. My brothers and I follow each other on social media, and they are married with kids. I call my brothers and their families on holidays and birthdays, but that's just about it. Thinking back, I realize how lucky I am to have my siblings still alive, and a part of me wants to reach out to work on our relationship, but my mother has always been in the back of my mind. My mother wasn't too happy about my father having outside children, as she likes to say, and didn't try to build a relationship, and whenever I spoke of them, she got upset, so I stopped.

Gianna calms down, and we cuddle in bed until we fall asleep again. The next time we wake up, it's almost 10am, and I reach out to find both Gianna and Luca aren't in bed anymore. I hear talking and smell food, and I lay down for a few more minutes until my stomach rumbles, and I get up and walk to the kitchen. Luca and Gianna are talking and finishing breakfast, and I wash my hands and set the table. The three of us have gotten into a rhythm when we are together and ensure no one person has more responsibilities than the other. We sat and ate, and they cooked pancakes, eggs, turkey bacon, and they open the smoked salmon. Lately, I have been leaning towards seafood more than red meat. I haven't determined if I want to go full pescetarian, but I have reduced the amount of other meat in my diet. When we finished breakfast and cleaned up, it's already 11:30am, and we got ready for the day. I decide to wear a plain fitted red t-shirt and yoga pants with pockets, and Gianna is wearing a green long-sleeve dress that extenuates her curves.

Luca is wearing a graphic T-shirt and some sweats. I head towards Luca's office after kissing both Luca and Gianna goodbye. Luca is taking Gianna to do the paternity test with her niece to have a recent one to show her parents. I stayed behind to get caught up on homework. I have 4 more months left in my semester, and this semester seems longer than the previous semesters. Luca asked me a few days ago what I wanted to do with my degree, and I mentioned I wanted to work in the finance department. He mentioned he would see what he could do. Still, I demanded to go through the entire hiring process like everyone else because I didn't want anyone to think I got handed the position. I open my Facebook messenger and message my brothers in our group chat to start a conversation. I am lucky enough to have my brothers still alive, and I want to work on our relationship while we still have time.

I get ahead of my homework, and my brothers and I have been texting back about our father and what's going on in our lives. According to my older brother Eduardo, 39 years old, plans to visit our father and discuss the possibility of him moving with Eduardo and his family. He got a job in Edinburgh, Scotland, and his new home has an in-law unit. My brothers have been unaware of our father's financial situation, but they have expressed their willingness to assist in his care. My second brother, Santiago 38, recently moved to Canada with his family a few weeks ago for a new job opportunity. The conversation went better than expected, and we realized how out of touch we all have been in each other's lives and promised to keep in touch at least once or twice weekly. I finally shut down my computer and saw that it's 1:45pm, and I texted Gianna to get an update. She responds that the paternity test is done, and results will be ready in a few days, and they are on their way back to the condo. Gianna also said they planned to go to Frisco Freeze, and I asked that they pick me up a fish sandwich meal with a malted milkshake, and she said they would be home in a few minutes.

I head toward the living room, plop on the couch, and scroll through TikTok while waiting for Luca and Gianna to return. I hear the elevator coming up, and Luca and Gianna enter with hands full of food and milkshakes.

I get up and set the table, and we sit again for lunch. "Aniyah met with her ex-boyfriend,"

I choked a bit. "Why would she do that?"

Gianna pats my back. "She wanted to close the chapter and tell him once and for all that she was done with him. Aniyah never got closure and wanted to get everything off her chest and move forward."

Luca puts his milkshake down. "I should text Seamus to see how he feels,"

Gianna finishes her bite. "No need. He met her at the restaurant, and they both walked out together; they are spending the rest of the day together."

I sip on my milkshake, glad that the meeting ended well and that Seamus and Aniyah are still together.

"So I have something to talk to you guys about,"

Luca and I put down our meals and looked at Gianna. "My lease is ending at the end of February, and I know this is probably too soon, but my roommates and I decided not to renew. My father handles my lease, and I could easily find another apartment alone, but I wondered if we three should move in together."

The room remains silent. Luca breaks the silence. "That's a big step for us, and I think we are ready for it. How do you guys feel?"

I think for a minute about our relationship and ask myself if the three of us are ready to move in together. I've known Luca for years, and when we started dating, I always saw myself moving in with him. With Gianna, she was unexpected, but she fit in like the perfect piece to our puzzle now; when I think of my future, I can't think of one without her. I have fallen for her quickly, and she has become my lover and my best friend. I look around the table and see both Luca and Gianna must be thinking about the question.

I already know my answer and want to lay it out. "I think we are ready. I love you, Luca, and have fallen fast for Gianna. I can't think of a future without you both, and moving in together is necessary to move our relationship forward."

The continued silence is making my heart beat faster; these past 3 weeks have shown me they feel the same way, or I hope that's what I have been seeing. Gianna breaks the silence again. "I've spent wasted time on dating apps hoping to find that special one, and I believe I have found it with you both. You guys don't judge me about how I want my future to look. In this short time, you guys have been my rock lately, and after the first week, I knew I loved both of you. I want to move in because I agree with Jaime that moving in will be a necessary step in our relationship, and judging by Luca's expression, I believe he feels the same way."

"I want a future with both of you, and I think it's settled. We are moving in together. So the next step is, where are we moving?"

Gianna

We spent the rest of the night discussing where we would want to live. Luca owns his condo, and Jaime and I's leases are ending soon, so we agreed for the time being to move in with Luca and put some of our items in storage. We also discussed finding a place that all three of us agree on and finances. My father has been paying my rent, so I have a nest egg saved up and can contribute to the new place. Still, my salary is significantly less than Luca and Jaime, and they have agreed to take on most of the finances, and I can cover utilities and other incidentals. We also needed to discuss what my future at my place of employment would look like. Luca briefly mentioned he was fine with me quitting, staying home, or working part-time at a daycare. Jaime seconded the motion, and it was getting late, so we tabled the conversation and went to bed.

I am awoken by kisses along my neck and a hand traveling down my body. I roll over and see Luca, and I kiss him back, and he pulls me onto him to straddle him. I lean down and continue to kiss him as his hands rub my ass. Luca reaches up, pulls my head wrap off, and runs his hands through my hair to undo my braid. My hair falls in a curtain on either side of my face, and Luca flips us again, careful not to wake Jaime. He grabs the bottom of my shirt and lifts it, exposing my breasts, and he leans down, takes a breast in my mouth, and circles my nipple with his tongue. I bite my lip to stifle a moan as he moves to the second breast, gives it the same treatment, and then kisses a line down my stomach. When he reaches my pussy, he teases my clit, and I let out a breathy moan and attempt to buck my hips, and Luca holds me down with one hand. He gives my clit one last lick, and I climax. I tried to keep from being loud, but I couldn't help it, and we looked over. Jaime was still sleeping and rolled over. Luca takes off his boxers, grabs his dick with one hand, and presses it to my entrance.

Luca pushes forward, holds one of my legs, and places it on his shoulder. Luca starts off slowly and then picks up the pace while leaning over me, hitting a deeper spot than before. Luca places a hand on my stomach and moves his hand up to my throat, and applies just enough pressure. I feel my second orgasm building, and it takes a few more thrusts, and my orgasm hits, and I cannot remain quiet, and Luca follows me over.

Luca pulls out and cuddles behind me while Jaime wakes. She cuts on the light and looks at the both of us. "Looks like the two of you had an entertaining morning."

I smile, and I can only assume Luca is smiling behind me. Jaime leans over, gives me a kiss, leans over me with her breasts in my face, and gives Luca a kiss too.

"What time is it, Jay?"

Jaime turns on her phone. "Oh wow, it's so early; it's 8am, and I think when we are bright-eyed and bushy-tailed, we should go over our group finances and our next steps."

I groan. "We can do that, but let's get some more sleep in first; come cuddle with us."

I open my arms, and Jaime takes off the sleep shirt she was wearing to bed and lays in my arms. I play with Jaime's breast, and she moans as I kiss her neck. I hear Luca lightly snoring behind me, and Jaime and I have sex until we are tired. The next time we awaken is when my phone rings.

I climb over to Jaime and hit the answer button. "This is Gianna.,"

"Good morning, Ms. Guzzo, this is Sara from Heartcore DNA Lab.,"

I stand up. "Yes, hello, are you calling about the results?"

"Yes, Ms. Guzzo, I wanted to tell you the results came back, that Nova Ricci is your niece. I will call her next to tell her the results. Do you have questions?"

"No, thank you so much for calling.," I hang up and look over to Luca and Jaime, who are sitting up waiting for the results. "It's confirmed she is my niece. I just need to speak to my parents about it."

A weight seems to lift from my shoulders, and I'm even more conflicted about how I feel about Nova. Fabi having a daughter is awesome, but it's heartbreaking he's not here to watch her grow. I'm so annoyed he didn't reach out for help and ended his life, forcing us to cope with the aftermath. I'm ashamed for being mad at Fabi for killing himself and leaving an emptiness in our family that'll never be filled. I am also sad that Fabi thought he couldn't reach out to get help and felt like the only solution he had was death. I need to reach out to a therapist to sort out these thoughts; while in my thoughts, I didn't realize Jaime and Luca looked at me with worried expressions.

"I'm okay, sort of, or I will be once I figure out my emotions."

Jaime gets out of bed and hugs me, and Luca kisses the top of my head and heads to the bathroom to start the shower. I returned my phone to the side table and saw Nova's texted me. She also got the call. I follow Jaime into the bathroom, shower, and prepare for the day.

Once dressed for the day, I text Aniyah to see if she wants a girl's dinner. She responds yes, and we agree to meet at Farelli's in Point Ruston at 6pm. Jaime, Luca, and I go to Luca's office and get started with our budget. We all write our budgets in separate spreadsheets and look at the budgets we created once we are done.

	Income	Housing cost	Utilities	Investments	Miscellaneous	Savings
Luca	$25,000	$7,000+ $300 condo association fees	$120	$10,000	$2,000	$5,580
Jaime	$10,000	$2500	$120	$2,000	$1,700	$3,680
Gianna	$3,360	$736 (dad covers it)	$50 (dad covers it)	Dad invests for her $5k	$1,800	$1,560

Looking at our budgets, my income pales compared to Jaime and Luca's, which I already knew before we created the budget.

"Looking at the budget, Jaime and I can cover the monthly expenses and still have enough to support you if you want to quit your job."

I think about it and am tempted to take their offer. I saved up a good nest egg with my dad, paying for everything. Currently, in my savings, I have over $75,000, so I can take care of my things and be just fine, plus my parents are always willing to help. I am not attached to my job and wouldn't mind quitting it once and for all.

"I have savings that can help with expenses; I don't love my job and want to leave, but I want to quit at the end of this month and be free of this job by the beginning of March."

Jaime chimes in, "you can quit. I agree with Luca; we have more than enough to take care of you and just want you to be happy.,"

She reaches over and rubs my leg. "I feel weird to just quit and be the stay-at-home girlfriend. I know we all said we see each other in our futures, but I don't want it to seem like I am taking advantage of you guys,"

Luca gets up from behind his computer, sits on the couch in his office, and pats his leg.

I placed my laptop on the desk, went over to him, sat in his lap, and Jaime joined us on the couch. "If we didn't want this, we wouldn't offer you this option. We initially knew what you wanted for your future and accepted all of you, including your plans."

Jaime leans on us. Luca wraps one arm around her middle. "You can quit; just let us know what you decide to do; in the meantime, we need to discuss what our living situation will look like. We got through our budget before we got off-topic again. I, for one, am tired of apartment living and want to get an actual home." Luca rubs my back with his other arm.

"I agree with Jaime, and I want a house with a yard that we don't have to worry about upstairs or downstairs neighbors or associations."

"Well, my mortgage has about $50,000 left to pay off, but if we play our cards right, we will sell the condo, make a profit, and put that towards purchasing a new home."

My nest egg will cover the rest of the mortgage, and I can afford to sacrifice it if that means we can move quicker. Paying off the rest of the mortgage is the least I can do to contribute to our household.

"I have over $70,000 saved because my dad has been paying for most of my expenses. I can pay off the rest of the mortgage, and we would be clear to purchase our new home."

Which gets both of them to look at me. "I don't want you using up your savings to pay the rest of my mortgage. I can handle my mortgage. Whenever I have a good year in the stock market, I use it to pay down my mortgage faster. Technically, I have savings that could pay for it. I haven't dipped into it in case anything happens with my business or health."

"I vote she does it she is offering and has the money to do so. It will allow her to pitch into finding a new home and allow you to keep your savings so we can continue building our future."

We go back and forth, and finally, Luca agrees to allow me to pay his mortgage. I check the time and see it's getting close to 6, and I head to the bedroom to get my purse for dinner with Aniyah.

Jaime walks behind me. "Do you want me to drop you off? I know how crazy parking is over by Point Ruston. I can also pick you up so you can drink."

"Thanks, Jay, if you don't mind."

Jaime and I head down to her car, and she drives me to the restaurant, where Aniyah stands outside waiting for me. I kiss Jaime, and she waives outside the window to Aniyah, and she and I embrace. We find a seat on the second floor on the patio; the waitress comes by, and we order wine and look through the menu.

"So, heifer, when were you going to tell me you were meeting with your ex? Also, Seamus was just cool with you meeting with the asshole?"

Aniyah laughs. "So he was mad when we got alone that I met with my ex only because he felt someone should've been with me because he didn't trust my ex. He calmed down a bit and asked me to move in with him, and I said yes."

The waitress came by, and we split a Mediterranean pizza and Farelli firesticks, and the waitress took our menus. It is unnaturally cool on a February night, but the weather has been funky in Washington this year, and we have to take the good days when they come.

"Congratulations, I'm so happy you are in a healthy relationship. I was so worried for you after your ex, and I'm glad you found a man like Seamus. Speaking of moving in, Jaime, Luca, and I will move in together at the end of my lease, and they mentioned I could quit the job if I wanted to. I'm considering quitting at the end of this month and filing an EEOC complaint about my supervisor."

The waitress came by again to drop off some water. Aniyah reaches her hand across the table. "I'm happy for you, too; this year has been strange, but I didn't have both of us finding love on my bingo card."

I laughed, and we resumed our conversation, and we had a refill on our wine, and our food came out next. "It's getting late, and we have work; we better call our significant others to pick us up. Do you want Luca or Jaime to drop you off since we are heading in that direction?"

Aniyah handles the bill with the waitress and responds, "If you can, Seamus is busy with a project, and I would hate to disrupt him."

I texted the group chat that we were ready, and Jaime responded Luca was already on the way to pick us up, and she texted Luca probably wouldn't mind dropping Aniyah off along the way.

We took the elevator back down to the main floor and walked arm and arm to a spot that was easy for Luca to spot us. I see Luca's Lexus pulling up, and he gets out to open the door for Aniyah and me and returns to the driver's side. We take less than 10 minutes to drop Aniyah off at Seamus's house. Seamus is waiting outside for her, and we wave at them and head back to Luca's condo. It's so weird to call it Luca's condo now that Jaime and I are moving in temporarily until we find a new place. The city lights pass us as The Weeknd plays on the radio, and Luca grabs my hand while keeping the other hand on the steering wheel. We get home in record time because of the lack of traffic, and I lean on Luca as we go up to our floor.

When we enter, Jaime is cleaning up in the kitchen, and I head to the bedroom to change and get ready for bed.

When I was done, I called my mom, who picked up on the second ring, "Hi baby, how are you?"

"Hey Mama, I'm just calling to check up on you."

My mom then explains that she and my dad are planning a trip to Nairobi in March. She details the upcoming trip. "Now that I am done talking about our trip, what's going on with you? You rarely call so late."

I take a deep breath. "Well, mama, I need to speak to you and Dad about something, but I need to do it in person. Can I come to visit you guys this Friday?"

"Sure, you can come anytime, but should I be worried that you want to speak in person?"

"No, mama, it's nothing wrong; I just need to talk to you guys face to face."

"Okay, I will get you a first-class ticket on Delta and email you the ticket."

"Thank you. I will see you on Friday night. I love you"

"Love you too"

We hang up, and I take a deep breath and look up to see Luca standing in the doorway. "I think it's a good idea to speak to them face to face. I can take you to the airport."

"Do you think they will react well to the news? They have avoided talking about him for so long that I worry about their reactions."

Luca steps into the room and sits on the bed beside me. "You never know until you tell them; plus, you speak about your parents; it sounds like they loved your brother and would be glad to know he has a daughter. They can be grandparents, too."

I leaned on his shoulder. "I hope this is the right thing to do because I would hate bringing this up, and it makes things worse."

"This could be beneficial for everyone, and maybe everyone can learn how to cope with their grief and heal correctly."

He kisses my forehead and gets up to get ready for bed, and Jaime comes in and does the same, and we get into bed, set the alarm and turn off the lights.

This week quickly passed without significant events, and I talked to Nova and Nova's mother Mattea. The conversation went as well as expected. Mattea is going through a hard time with her divorce and trying to reconnect with Nova. When Nova discovered the facts, she was mad at her mom, and they resorted to family therapy to tackle some disagreements they were having. She was receptive to speaking with my parents and allowing them to meet Nova, but she needs time before meeting with them, which is understandable. After work on Friday, Luca and Jaime pick me up with my suitcase in the trunk, and we head to SeaTac airport. They drop me off, and I board the plane preparing for what's to come. My dad waits for me outside the airport and helps me with my luggage, and we drive back to my childhood home. We spend the night having a family dinner and watching a movie together. I determined it was best to do it tomorrow since we plan to take a beach trip to San Diego and stay at our beach home.

We get up early, load the car, and make the drive to San Diego. As we drove, I told them about my relationship and my apartment plans. They're not super thrilled about me living with Jaime and Luca, but they'll stand behind me and they'd like to meet them. We arrive at the beach house, unpack, get dressed in bathing suits, and head out to the backyard space that extends onto the beach, and now is the right time to talk to them about Nova. I was nervous as I sat near my parents.

I breathed in deep to calm myself so I could talk. "Mom, Dad, there's something I need to tell you."

My parents looked at me, curious and concerned. "I don't know how to say this, but it's about Fabiano," I say hesitantly.

My parents looked at each other in confusion. "What about Fabiano, honey?" my mother questions, gently touching my leg.

"He has a daughter," I blurts out, relieved I didn't have to hold this secret anymore.

"A daughter? What do you mean?" my father asks, his face contorting with confusion.

"I found out a few weeks ago. Fabiano had gotten a woman pregnant before he passed." I revealed that when his daughter Nova was born, the mother Mattea was married, so she allowed her husband to think that Nova was his.

There was a moment of silence as my parents processed the news. "Why didn't he tell us?" my mother asks, breaking the silence.

"I don't know. Maybe Fabi was ashamed to admit to you guys that he had an affair with a married woman. He was already struggling with his mental health, so there could be multiple reasons he hid it," I reply, shrugging my shoulders.

My father runs his hands through his hair. "This is a lot to take in. Are you sure Nova is Fabiano's daughter?"

"Yes, I recently did a DNA test, and it came back that she is my niece, but Mattea also alleges that she and Fabi did a DNA test before his passing, so he knew before he died." My mom was in tears and my dad was just as shocked as I was when I heard.

"Why didn't you tell us when you first found out?"

I look at my father. "Because you and Mom spent years not talking about him, and when I brought him up, it only upset you guys. So I've been pretending I don't remember him, but I do; I remember everything about him and miss him daily. Pretending I don't remember him to protect your feelings has been hard. I can't and won't do it any longer."

Tears are running down my face, my voice is cracking, and through tears, I see my mother crying. My dad looked sad.

My mom composed herself enough to answer, "Oh honey, I am so sorry you have had to pretend you didn't remember Fabiano. When you said you couldn't remember him, we decided it was best to take down his pictures and move on so we wouldn't have to keep reminding you of your brother's death. We miss him daily and feel guilty that we weren't there for your brother when he struggled. We only wanted the best for you and your brother/ when your brother neglected his responsibilities and dropped out of law school, we thought tough love would help put him on the right track again. You may not remember, but your brother wasn't working and spending so much money on drugs, and we argued with him a lot. We tried everything, but nothing worked; after his death, we found his journals and found out he was hearing voices and having severe mood swings."

My father finishes. "Fabiano's mother had a history of bipolar disorder, but it was being treated. When she passed in the car accident, she had no contact with her family, so I didn't know if anyone else had it. I thought I was looking for the right signs and didn't need to get him professional help, which is one of my biggest regrets. I should have had him seen by a therapist to make a professional diagnosis."

The information overload is a lot, but this conversation is long overdue, and I am glad this is happening. "Mattea will allow Nova to meet you guys, but if you want to meet her, I am considering going to therapy to help sort through all of this."

"That's a good idea, and I think your father and I need to go through therapy,"

My mother looks at my dad. "I agree. I thought we had healed from his death, but much more work needs to be done."

The tension that filled the space lifts, and we got up from the spot we were sitting and went further down the beach and spent the rest of the day talking about Fabiano, and for once in my life, I felt like we were all healing.

Luca

I am sitting down behind my computer working on some work projects when I receive a group text message from Gianna told us the conversation went well, and that she is flying back Sunday night. Jaime sends a dancing emoji with a heart, and I also send a heart. I return to my work, and I run my hands through my hair. Taking in the current screen, a headache is developing. The company we bought two years ago had some flawed business dealings and was in danger of going bankrupt. I am working with Jasmine to discover how to save this company. Jasmine reminded me we would not be responsible for the company's creditors if it went under. However, that is not how I operate when a subsidiary is having troubles; I try to mediate a merger or find investors to save the company. I cannot find any investors, and the next solution is to merge them with another subsidiary. Seamus trained Jasmine well, and she found 3 companies in better financial shape and could take a merger with this company. We now have to work out a deal that works for everyone, and deals get sticky when egos and money are involved. Glancing at the clock on my phone, Jasmine and I realize it is nearing 4 pm, and we decide to end our work for the day since nothing more could be accomplished.

I decide to call Seamus to catch up with him, seeing as we both have been busy and haven't had a minute to talk. Seamus doesn't pick up when I first call, and I call again, and he picks up,

"Hey bro, what's up?"

"Nothing much, just trying to catch up with my little bro seeing how we haven't had a minute to chat,"

"Well, I'm pretty sure Jaime and Gianna keep you up to date, but Aniyah and I are moving in together temporarily. Then we will go house hunting in Seattle, and nothing much has been happening other than talking to our mother and trying to tell her you are just busy, and that's why you haven't called in a minute."

I cringed at the statement and realized that I hadn't called my mom in about 3 weeks, and I wrote a note to call my mother. My mother knows that I am more difficult to reach than my brother because of the company taking most of my available time, and Gianna and Jaime taking what's left.

"Yea, I can admit I haven't been the best son lately. I will call Mom this week."

"Speaking of this week, Jasmine has been doing great lately and has been taking on more responsibilities. She seems ready to lead."

I figured this conversation would happen eventually and Seamus has kept up his side of the deal, and he's right. Jasmine is pretty much independent of Seamus. When we made this deal, my father and I agreed to invest in his literary café if he trained a replacement, so I wasn't left without a lawyer.

Based on the revenue we have been bringing in, I can invest in half of Seamus's business. "I knew this conversation was coming, but Jasmine has been valuable to the company. Dad and I said a year, but I feel you have met your end of the deal, so I will talk to Dad."

I hear a loud yell on the other end, "Thank you, big bro. I swear you will not regret it. I can stay until the end of the month to close out my affairs and officially quit."

I'm genuinely happy for my brother that he is getting to follow his dreams. I will be sad that I won't see him every day in the office, but he needs to take this step; when I was building my company, he was there since the beginning. He helped me build my company to where it is now and helped me achieve my dreams; now it's time for me to do the same for him. We talk for a couple more minutes before we hang up, and I get up and head toward the living room to see what Jaime is up to. She has her headphones in and is working on her computer, probably her coursework, utterly oblivious to the world. I crouch down and quietly approach her, staying behind her so she doesn't spot me.

I reach out and grab her waist when I get behind her chair. "Boo!"

She lets out a loud scream and aims an elbow in my direction, but I predicted that and could move out of the way before she connected. Laughing, I looked at her, and the reaction on her face showed she wasn't amused by my little joke.

"Really, I thought you grew out of that."

" Laughing, I say, "Never." I move to bring her into a hug, and she allows it. "Let me make it up to you. I can take you to dinner at Kizuki Ramen & Izakaya, your favorite Ramen by the mall, and then take you out for boba."

She weighs my suggestion, "If you make it a crumble cookie, I'll forgive you." "Done." She grins and makes her way to the bedroom to switch her outfit.

I head to the guest bathroom, fix my hair, and hear Jaime down the hall. "I'm ready."

I walk in her direction, speechless. Jaime has freed her blond hair from the ponytail I saw earlier, and she has curled it. She is wearing a green sweater dress that hugs her curves and has brown knee-high boots. Jaime looked as stunning as ever when we were in high school. I used to remember her talking about wanting plastic surgery to have bigger breasts, hips, and butt, and we always told her she was fine the way she was. She is still beautiful, and she blushes when she catches me admiring her.

"So, is my handsome date going to show me to his car?"

She holds out a hand, and I take it and kiss it. " Of course, my lady."

We make our way to my Lexus in the garage, and I open the door, help her in the passenger side, and go around and get in the driver's side. Reaching the restaurant doesn't take long, and we walk inside to get seated. During dinner, we discuss our day and the upcoming week. Jaime was excited to graduate in May, and she spoke with her advisor, who told her she would graduate with honors. I'm proud of her and what she is accomplishing. Jaime didn't follow the same path as Seamus, and I did after high school. We were lucky enough to have the privilege of going to college and get our advanced degrees debt free. Jaime worked hard in high school, but it wasn't enough to pay for school. When she started working for me, she showed an interest in getting her bachelor's, and I offered to pay for her degree. After delaying it for a few years, Jaime got accepted into UW and now graduation is around the corner. When she graduates, I told her I would want her in a new position and would need her to train her replacement.

Dinner went well, and we drove to Crumble Cookie, got 2 cookies each, and shared. We got home around 8pm and re-watched Star Wars, The Phantom Menace. She and I are fans of the prequel trilogy, while Gianna loves the original movies. While watching the film, a notification goes off on my work phone, and I ignore it because if employees need me, they need to call if I don't answer the text message.

Three more notifications go off on my work phone, and Jaime looks over. "That's weird; if it's an emergency, why aren't they calling?"

I shrug my shoulder, and another notification comes again. I huff and put the movie on pause. "Let me see what's going on."

I unwrap from around Jaime's shoulder and reach to pick my phone up. I see Hillary's name; she has sent multiple text messages, and I reluctantly open the messages. Jaime looks over my shoulder, and we gasp at what we see. Hillary's in Gianna's place, wearing black, and she's got a match and lighter fluid. The following texts are pictures of the apartment on fire and a view from across the street showing flames coming out of the unit's window and the fire spreading up. The last message is a video of the fire department working to put the fire out. I am absolutely shocked at how stupid she is to send us evidence of her committing a crime.

"Does she lack common sense, or is she just bold? She just sent proof of her committing arson. Also, we need to contact Gianna's roommates to ensure they weren't home."

"You contact her roommates, and I will call the police and send the information over. I'm a little concerned with her mental state if she willingly sends proof of committing a crime, and I don't think we should stay here in case she gets the idea to set fire to my place."

Jaime looks at me. "I guess you are right, but if the police catch her, we shouldn't worry, right?"

"Mhmm, even if they can lock her up tonight, we don't know if she has an accomplice."

Jaime nods, and we both start making calls and heading to the bedroom. We loaded up our bags and a few of Gianna's items and I'm sure she'll be furious when she finds out her belongings burned up. Jaime contacted Gianna's roommates to confirm that they weren't home when the fire happened. They both had events tonight and got pissed when they realized they didn't have a place to stay. I offered to book them a hotel suite in downtown Tacoma and take care of the cost. They accepted, and Jaime followed up by calling Gianna, who sounded tired to inform her of the news and she, like her roommates, was upset that she doesn't have an apartment anymore. Gianna changed her ticket and will come in at midnight instead of tomorrow night, which her parents rightfully understood. Gianna said she could take a Lyft to the hotel we were going to be staying, and Jaime and I insisted on being there to pick up, and not wanting to fight, she accepted.

We get settled into the hotel suite, and the police call me back, requesting my location. I provided them with the hotel address, met with them to discuss the situation, and mentioned they were looking for Hillary. According to the police, since I fired Hillary a week ago, they learned that her former friends at the job filed restraining orders. According to the report, Hillary got mad when they didn't come to her defense and became violent to the point she attacked one of them. The police also said that her violence has escalated since then. Hillary refused to leave after a company she was interviewing with found out why she lost her job. She alleged that they unfairly discriminated against her because she was a woman. When the interviewer explained it was because of the harassment allegation, she became irate and threatened to stab the interviewer. Jaime was indifferent to the news, considering Hillary gave her a difficult time when she was working for me.

I am worrying about her welfare because I never envisioned her being so belligerent; The police asked if I wanted to press charges against her for the forced kiss, and I declined, not wanting to add to her legal woes. It really irritated Jaime about her car and the break in, yet she didn't want to take any legal action and wanted to sever ties with Hillary right away. The police leave, and Jaime and I unpack and I check the suite to ensure that we are safe. It's 10pm and we have another hour before we have to pick Gianna up from the airport and we used the time to look at houses. I know Seamus and Aniyah are looking for homes in the Seattle area, but Gianna, Jaime and I love the Tacoma area. A few years ago, I floated the idea of moving the business to Tacoma from Auburn, but that idea never came to fruition. It's not entirely off the table, and I am pretty sure most employees would be thankful if we moved. It would cut some commutes in half. The surrounding areas have significantly gone up in price, forcing all the employees to move south of Auburn. My alarm signals that it is time we make our way to SeaTac to collect Gianna. Jaime and I make our way to my car and she attempts to get in the driver's side before I tell her I will drive. We make the commute to SeaTac and we arrive right on time and have to wait another 20 minutes before we see Gianna exiting the airport. I exited the car, took her luggage, and drove back to the hotel. Gianna falls asleep immediately once she gets in. When we arrive at the hotel, I park in the valet area and carry Gianna to our suite. Jaime and I change into sleepwear and I help to remove Gianna's clothing and we all turn in for the night.

I hear my ringtone and I decline the call and roll over and lay my arms over Jaime and Gianna. When my phone rings for the second time, I give up trying to go back to sleep and unlock my phone to see it's an unknown number.

Picking up "Hello this is Luca," the line is quiet and I check my phone to make sure the phone didn't hang up. I repeat, "Hello this is Luca. Who is this?"

"Hi Luca, this is Hillary. I messed up big time, and I don't have anyone else to call.,"

I am stunned for a moment, not understanding why Hillary would call me. "Why are you calling me? You broke into Jaime's apartment, you pushed yourself onto me, and now you set fire at Gianna's apartment."

The line goes quiet again and I hear a sniffle. "I know I have royally screwed up recently, but I haven't been feeling well. My mind has been racing. I try not to listen to the voice in my head, but the voice won't quiet down. But when I do what they say, the voices stop. I don't know what's wrong with me. Please help me."

I can hear her desperation in her voice, but I'm now suspicious if this is genuine or not. Going against my better judgment, "where are you? Jaime and I can meet you,"

She sniffles. "Jaime hates me. Why would she help?"

I sigh "because she has a heart, and she doesn't hate you. She dislikes you, but doesn't hate you."

She rattles off her address which isn't far from where we are and Gianna and Jaime are already awake and putting on clothes "this is a terrible idea but we aren't letting you meet her alone" Jaime marches to the closet and throws my t-shirt and jeans on the bed.

We're dressed and in the car in record time, and Gianna is on the phone with the detective to explain the situation. It doesn't take long for us to arrive at Hillary's location. She is in Point Ruston on the pier, looking over the side. I approach her and she hears me coming and turns around. Hillary has always kept herself put together. I haven't seen her dressed casually in years.

The Hillary that is standing in front of me is unrecognizable with tears in her eyes. "You came.,"

I maintain distance between us. "Yes, you called in distress. You know the police are looking for you and you have committed arson."

"It wasn't me, it was the voices made me do it. I have been trying to ignore them the past few years, and I have been able to do it, but they just have gotten louder.," She is now crying. "I am sorry, but I don't know what to do. My parents and siblings are not speaking to me because I brought shame onto them and my friends fear me."

In the corner of my eye, I see Jaime approaching. "Hillary, you need help, but first you have to answer for what you have done. The police are coming and if you go with them, we can see about getting you a lawyer that can help get you the help you need."

She looks at Jaime. "I've caused such a mess. Why are you helping me?"

"Because before all of this you were the most selfless person and the Hillary that I know would spend her free time helping others so let us help you"

I hold out my hand as we hear sirens in the background. She takes my hand and hugs me, crying, and I rub her back. When the cops came, she agreed to go with them and true to her word, Jaime looks for attorneys. Once the police are gone, Jaime, Gianna and I make our way back to my car and head back to the hotel, glad that this fiasco is over with and that Hillary will get the help she needs.

Jaime

To say this past month has been crazy has been an understatement of the year. I held up to my end of my bargain and I found an amazing lawyer who took on her case and Hillary's lawyer plead no contest and the DA accepted. The sentencing was 3 years probation, mandatory mental health treatment, restitution, and she has to maintain full-time employment. Honestly, even after all that has happened between us, I'm glad that she avoided jail time and will get the mental health treatment she needs. Amidst the chaos, Gianna's roommates figured out alternative places to live. Rosie moved to California to take the new job offer, and we had a going away party for her. Jessie got engaged and her boyfriend proposed and they found a place in Federal Way and he will move in at the end of May after graduating. Gianna was beyond happy that her roommates were moving on in life, but was still sad when they went their separate ways. Aniyah and Seamus moved in together and Seamus quit his position at the company. We naturally had a going away party for him and he immediately started on progress for his literary café. I am about to complete my last semester, with my classes wrapping up in June and the commencement ceremony immediately after. For once, there appear to be no hiccups in my life.

This week is a flurry of emotions as Gianna resigns from her job and embarks on a new life as a stay at home girlfriend, a decision more beneficial than she realizes. One of her first tasks she wants to complete is narrowing down our housing choices and scheduling open houses. We have spent the last few weeks meticulously narrowing down our housing list to 4 choices that we all agree on. I am overwhelmed by a mixture of emotions as I begin therapy for the first time to confront my childhood wounds and undo the unhealthy patterns I assimilated from my parents. Growing up, the thought of seeing a therapist never occurred to me. My parents always have been against going to a therapist because it meant someone prying into house business. I think they both would benefit from their own therapy and maybe they will both unlearn the toxic coping mechanisms they learned from their parents. I have been postponing it out of fear of confiding in anyone outside of my inner circle, yet I think now is the right time to do it prior to the three of us forming a family. Luca and Gianna set up their own therapy sessions, and we all agreed to be accountable to each other.

I keep checking the clock at work and see it's 5:30pm and my therapy session is at 6:30pm in Tacoma. Luca has agreed to do most of the closing duties so that I can make it to my first session. Once I leave work, it takes at least 30 minutes to arrive at my therapist, Dr. Miller's office. I linger in the parking lot for another 15 minutes prior to entering the building, my uneasiness intensifying as I register and await my appointment. A friendly woman with gray hair and glasses opens the door and calls my name and I greet her and she shows me to a corner office with an amazing view and I sit on one couch and she takes a seat on the other couch facing me.

I survey the room as Dr. Miller flashes a smile. "Hello, Jaime. My name is Dr. Miller. It's a pleasure to meet you." Dr. Miller's calm and reassuring voice put me at ease. "This may not be easy for you, however, I am here to assist. There is no prescribed approach to begin therapy, so why not tell me what you want to tell me regarding yourself?"

My nerves ease a little more and I tell her about my parents, my dad's deportation, and how life with my mother was. I got emotional when talking and Dr. Miller hands me napkins as I continue. Dr. Miller listened intently, nodding her head and took notes. She asked gentle questions to encourage me to keep talking and to help me explore my thoughts and feelings. As I spoke more and more, I experienced a wave of relief. I felt the weight I had been shouldering for all these years slowly lift from my shoulders.

Eventually, the session ended. Dr. Miller thanked me for sharing my story. Just before I left, Dr. Miller put emphasis on the fact that healing is a lengthy process, and she showed she would be available if I desired to continue with her. I scheduled a follow-up appointment with her the following Monday. As I walked out of the office, I felt a mixture of emotions—sadness, relief, vulnerability, and hope. Today marked a huge stride in my healing progress and to have a doctor I can confide in makes me feel less alone. I make the brief journey home and I am greeted with smells of enchiladas and my stomach growls.

Gianna and Luca are sitting on the couch watching TV, and Gianna turns her head. "I left your dinner in the stove for you and we can talk after you eat if you are up to it."

I pass the couch and lean down to kiss Gianna, then Luca, and head to the kitchen to prepare my dinner.

I shared with Gianna and Luca about my therapy session and my feelings soon after dinner, and they stated they were glad I got on well with my therapist. I headed to the bedroom, and they stayed out in the living room to continue watching TV. Peering at the clock, I realize that it's only 9pm and my mother should be up and a mysterious impulse causes me to phone her.

She picks up, and we said pleasantries and she stops speaking. "Mija, you sound distracted. What's on your mind? Is it your relationship? I told you, maybe this polyamorous thing wasn't the best idea. Relationships are supposed to be monogamous."

I roll my eyes. Luca and Gianna's parents have approved our relationship, even my father, but my mother is having a hard time coming to terms with our relationship. She expressed that our relationship is unnatural any chance she had. I told her that if she kept expressing her thoughts, our conversation would be limited and she has not voiced her sentiments since then. "No, it's not about my relationship. It is fine. I had my first therapy session today, and it felt good."

The line goes quiet and I make sure it didn't disconnect. "Why would you go to a complete stranger and tell your business to them? How can you trust this doctor won't use what you say to put you in the hospital?"

I take a deep breath. My mother has some views on therapy, and one view is that if you speak too much to a therapist, they will commit you against your will. "Mom, for the last time, a therapist will not commit you unless you are a danger to yourself or someone else. Even at that they can't force you to go, but to answer your question, it felt good to talk to someone about everything and have them listen and help me through those emotions."

"I don't think this is a good idea and I don't support this, but you are an adult, so you can make your own decision," I huff. I figured she wouldn't support me. She always has to be so difficult. We talk for a little while before I said goodnight and hung up the phone.

Gianna

June

The preceding three months have been a maelstrom of feelings, both pleasant and unpleasant. I resigned from my job at the call center, and Aniyah soon followed suit. I filed an EEOC complaint against my previous supervisor and further female coworkers provided corroboration for the complaint. Several of my former colleagues and I stayed in touch, and I heard rumors they terminated him immediately after the truth was exposed and the atmosphere of that division improved. The three of us have seen a positive effect from therapy, taking part in some group sessions, which has led to an incredible transformation in our relationship. I felt our relationship was stable, yet engaging in therapy enabled us to better our communication tactic. I coordinated a meeting with Nova and my parents with permission from Mattea, and the meeting was emotional but incredible. During Nova's spring break, my parents showered her with love and we all visited our beach home in San Diego for a week. During that time, my parents engaged her in a discussion about Fabiano and gave replies to queries about the family lineage. It elated Nova when my mom and dad proposed taking her to Italy and Cameroon during the summer months. Nova coming into our family has caused a much needed shift and I believe she is healing the wounds of the past.

Jaime, Luca and I eventually stumbled upon the ideal house that we all consented to in Point Ruston, which is humorous considering that when we were settling in, Seamus and Aniyah were moving out. At one point, Jaime, Luca, and I considered Seattle as a potential home, but soon reverted to our original plan of staying in Tacoma. Our circumstances have changed, so Aniyah and I don't connect as much. Even though our lives are busy beyond belief, we attempt to stay in touch via text, and we strive to meet up in person at least once or twice a week when our calendars permit. This month was thrilling, because Jaime completed her bachelor's degree, and I organized a sizeable celebration with our families to mark her accomplishment. With some reluctance, I invited

Jaime's mother, who I know has no love for me, but she was polite enough to mask her dislike and she conducted herself well at the party. I was astounded that she didn't suffer a heart attack when Luca proposed a toast and kissed Jaime and myself. Jaime's father and siblings connected with us through video chat. Luca presented a graduation gift to her as a trip to visit her father and siblings and, because of Luca's lack of skill in organizing, I took care of the planning which Luca was thankful for.

I am sitting on the couch making a list of things that need to be done before the move. We plan to close and move in on July 8th and just looking at the list was already giving me a headache and I'm wondering if I can get this done. Occasionally, since quitting my job, I have contemplated if I am really supporting this relationship, but Jaime and Luca both state that my remaining at home has been helpful and they are thankful for all I contribute. I have assumed the responsibility of family secretary, and, despite the occasional pressure, I find pleasure in organizing our schedules and making sure everything is in its proper place. I observe the time on my phone and observe that it's close to 6:30pm and I note that neither Jaime nor Luca have returned home at this point and there has been no response to me from either of them, which is concerning. Just as I am about to dial either of them, I hear a rap at the door. Only family, friends, or strangers use the front door, but Jaime and Luca always use the elevator. I power off my computer and then proceed to the door to glance through the peephole and recognize it's Aniyah.

I open the door to see her hands are full of what looks like a dress and hair products. "We don't have much time. Grab this and we need to get ready."

She hands me her bag of hair products. Confused, I allow her in. "Get ready for what, exactly?"

She walks towards the bedroom without a response, and I close and lock the door. "Stop asking questions and come on."

Seeing that she isn't going to answer my questions, I follow her to the bedroom to get ready for whatever is going on. "Also, because I know you are going to ask Jaime and Luca are fine, Luca sent me here for a reason now come sit down"

She is standing at my make up dresser and pats the chair. I hang the dress on the door and sit. Aniyah presented me with a delicate makeup look after working her miracles on my hair. She walks over to the garment bag and unzips it and I see it is revealed to be a beautiful blue backless dress and my mouth hangs open.

"Well, don't stand there with your mouth open. You are going to catch flies hurry so I can help you dress."

I hurry over and Aniyah helps me into the gown and it fits like a glove and I bend down a little so she can help me put on a sapphire necklace with matching earrings. Aniyah fashioned my hair into a curly up do that I adore but cannot replicate myself.

She stands back to take in her work. "You look like a million bucks now let's go" because of the craziness I didn't see that Aniyah is wearing a cream jumpsuit with red heels and her hair is loose.

After I had donned my high heels, I trailed her down the elevator to her car, then I got in and we drove the short distance to Point Ruston near the movie theater. Upon our arrival, I spot Seamus stationed on the corner and he strides over to be of help to Aniyah and me from the car and steps into the driver's side to park; I presume. Aniyah requests I shut my eyes, and my heart flutters, anxious about what is going to happen, and I clasp her hand, and she leads me. Aniyah alerts me to the steps before us and we descend a flight of stairs, halting when I sense hands clasping my own. "Open your eyes. " I open to see Luca standing in front of me. I look around to see Jaime standing to the right of me, also dressed up. "Do you know what's going on?" I look at her, who seems just as confused as I am. Luca smiles. "I have something I want to say to the both of you, and it's about time I did." My heart is still fluttering.

"Gianna, when I first met you in McMenamins, I did not know the impact you would have on not only me but Jaime. Before you, I didn't know how to express my emotions and Jaime and I were struggling, unsure what our future looked like. I can't speak for Jaime, but when you came into my life, you taught me the importance of speaking up and recognizing my emotions. You fit into our life unexpectedly and even though we have been together for a short time, I can't imagine my life without you. Gianna Aria Guzzo will you marry me and commit to our relationship for the rest of our lives,"

Tears are streaming down my face and I nod my head and Luca kneels and takes out a ring that has three sapphires that are interlocking and puts it on my finger. I look over to Jaime and she has tears of joy as well and I kiss Luca and then Jaime.

"I am not done yet, Jaime. We have known each other almost all of our lives. You have been spitfire from the moment I met you and you reminded me of myself. Some would say that's a good thing, but others would say likes repel. When we started our relationship almost a year ago, we did not know what the future held for us. Like I said earlier, we hit a period where we were struggling, and Gianna came in and fit like a missing puzzle piece." Luca grabs my hand and pulls me to him. "You are my first love and best friend. I don't want to live this life without you, Jaime Selena Cabrera. Will you do the honor of marrying me and committing to this relationship?"

He releases me and kneels and pulls out a similar ring to mine but has rubies in it. She nods her head and just like that, we are all engaged. We hear clapping and Jaime and I turn and we see our friends and family standing on the steps and Luca pulls Jaime and me closer.

Our friends and family come down to surround us and congratulate us. As I take in the sight of Jaime and Luca, I feel an immense happiness knowing that we will soon be a family.

Jaime's mother smiled uneasily. "I should offer congratulations, yet one question lingers. Luca legally can only marry one of you - who will be the lucky one?"

She sips the champagne that was given out. I can't hide how I feel and neither could anyone else as the mother-in-law from hell ruined the proposal. Jaime's facial expression shifts. "You are correct, mother and if you must know, Luca is going to marry Gianna legally."

She triumphantly sips her champagne and her mother frowns. We have not even come close to figuring out the details of this event. We expected the engagement gathering to be simply celebratory, yet her mother could not pass up the chance to create a problem. But I am glad she responded without a second thought. It was always my assumption that Jaime and Luca would be the ones marrying legally and I held no objections with that, since we would still be united regardless, yet when Jaime proposed that Luca and I should wed, I was content with that too.

I could discern from her mother's expression that she wasn't happy with that declaration, yet understanding that voicing any more would jeopardize her relationship with Jaime, she simply agreed. The three of us celebrate until almost 11pm and everyone heads home for the night. When we arrive in the condo, Jaime grabs me and starts kissing me with her hands on my lower back and I return the kiss. Luca guides us to the bedroom and pushes us to the bed and Jaime lays back and I straddle her as Luca removes our heels. Jaime runs her hands up and down my bare back and pushes my dress down to expose my breast and stomach. I stand and slid the rest of the dress off and Jaime stands and does the same and Luca pulls up the chair by the window to the bed and takes a seat. Jaime then pushes me on to the bed and climbs on top of me and kisses me. I run my fingers through her hair, then down her back and she moves her hand down my stomach until she reaches my pussy and puts two fingers in. She teases me and uses her thumb to stroke my nub and I break the kiss to moan. She moves faster and lowers her head to take one breast in her mouth and uses her tongue to play with my nipple. I'm panting as she moves to the other breasts, and I turn my head to see Luca with his shirt unbuttoned and his dick in his hand rubbing up and down. I lick my lips and Luca stands and removes his shirt the rest of the way and takes his pants and boxers off. He steps in front of me with his dick in his hand and rubs his dick along my lower lip and I open to lick his dick. He grabs my hair and releases it from the up do and pushes inside my mouth and I gag a little. I no longer feel Jaime's fingers inside me. Luca puts his dick deep and continues until I feel liquid going down my throat and he removes his dick from my mouth.

Luca manipulates us like his little dolls and Jaime is laying on her back and I am between her open legs with my back arched. Without another word, I eat her out like the way she like, and Luca enters me from behind. I use my tongue to lavish her nub and she moans even louder and I move my hands up her stomach and cup her breast and roll her nipples between my fingers, eliciting a louder moan. Luca hits my sweet spot and while eating Jaime out, I moan. Sensing Jaime is close, I move my hand to use a combination of both tongue and fingers to bring her to climax. Luca reaches between us and uses his fingers to play with my nub and it only takes a short while until I follow Jaime to climax. Last, Luca follows the both of us and Luca lies on the bed, enveloping us in the covers and wrapping his arm around our waists and brings us closer. As I succumb to slumber, I reflect on my good fortune to have encountered Jaime and Luca and contemplate the possibilities in our collective future.

A week passes since the engagement, and we have been in an engagement bliss. Jaime's mother insisted that she should be the legally recognized wife as she was the one who entered the relationship first. Jaime's mother thinks there is a pecking order between the three of us and that Jamie's status should be superior to mine. Jaime has disregarded her mother's demands and we giggle at the idea of her mom imagining there is a rank in our relationship. During our dating period, we have implemented no kind of hierarchical structure and instead view our relationship as a partnership where we are both equal. Jaime has accepted a Financial advisor role inside Luca's company and the recently hired secretary has been showing remarkable proficiency in the role. Our real estate broker communicated to us we can conclude the closing process at the beginning of July, which is convenient as we plan to go to Barcelona in another week. I reserved a stunning villa to accommodate Jaime, Luca and myself, as well as Jaime's brothers, their families, and her father. Jaime knows we are going to spend time with her family, but she doesn't know that we will all be under the same roof. Prior to our departure next Friday, I have booked an appointment with my doctor. I am tired and it is unclear if this results from the work I am doing or something else entirely.

Luca

Gianna has been phenomenal with all the work she has devoted to this trip. She organized accommodations, planned excursions, and even organized an additional graduation celebration prior to our departure. Gianna and I arranged a 3-week vacation, and I have assigned tasks to a reliable employee. Since I started this business, I haven't taken much of a break, scared that my business would go under. We spent the night before flying packing our bags and I have noticed something has been off with her since her doctor's appointment earlier this week. She hasn't said anything to Jaime or me and I want to ask, but I want to give her time to tell us if something is wrong. I am going to give her until the end of this trip and if she hasn't said anything by then, I will ask her directly. On the day of our flight, we arrived at SeaTac earlier than expected, and to my amazement, Gianna had upgraded us from business to first class. I ordered 3 flutes of champagne to do a toast before take off. Gianna respectively declined and requested Ginger Ale and my mind goes to pregnancy. Jaime shoots me a glance and raises her eyebrow, signifying that she shares the same opinion. We have not delved into the subject of when to have kids, however both Jaime and Gianna have been on birth control, and I'm of the sentiment that if it were to come to pass, then that would be fine. Drawing closer to 40, I am now in a place to start a family.

International trips have always taken a toll on my body, and as I age, I felt it. We traveled from Seattle to Heathrow, and we had a day gap and Gianna secured us a hotel near the airport. She also planned for us to do a quick sightseeing trip in London, which was exciting because it was Jaime's first time to London. Jaime hasn't had the same travel opportunities as Gianna and me because of her parents' financial situation during her upbringing. Jaime had visited Spain a few times when her mother could manage it and when she began working for me, she made a few trips, however it was usually to the Caribbean. When we landed, a driver was waiting for us to take us to the villa and Gianna whispered that Jaime's family had already checked in and set up some balloons and the cook made Jaime's favorite foods. The trip to the villa took around one hour and when we showed up, it was breathtaking. I entrusted a lot of the planning to Gianna and gave her access to my bank account. After we got engaged, I opened a joint bank account where most of our monies went so that Gianna could pay bills and take care of needs. To prevent Jaime from discovering what we were doing, I provided Gianna with my banking details so that she could pay for everything from my account.

Jaime was so moved when she realized what we had arranged. She was delighted to have more opportunities to bond with her father and brother's families. We got introduced to Jaime's brothers and their families; we met Santiago, his wife Isabella, along with their son Kylan, and twins Dorothy and Dylan. Her oldest brother, Eduardo, introduced himself and his wife, Marie, their sons, Cooper, Daniel, and daughters, Gloria and Marianna. We enjoyed our dinner and afterwards gathered in the living room to take part in board and card games, lasting until the wee hours of the night. As the hour grew late, Jaime, Gianna and I said goodnight and went to our room. The room was spacious, featuring high ceilings, sweeping windows with a view of the hills, and a sizable bathroom. As we were unpacking, getting ready for sleep, Gianna rushed to the bathroom and I heard her vomiting. When Gianna ran to the bathroom, Jaime went after her in and was holding her hair back and rubbing her back. I rummaged through the cabinet in search of medicine and a cup for water. Once she was done, I have pinpointed a cup and Jaime asked if Gianna needs a doctor. Jaime is fishing in her pocket for her phone.

Clasping Jaime's arm, Gianna utters, "you don't need to call a doctor. I already know why I got sick."

Gianna stands and walks past me to the basin and starts brushing her teeth. I held my hand out to help Jaime up and we waited for her to continue brushing. Jaime and I briefly exchanged a confused stare, and we accompanied Gianna to our cozy seating spot by the window. "I have been feeling under the weather for a few weeks. Earlier this week, I visited the doctor, and she confirmed I'm pregnant and the baby is due in February."

I was already ready for this because of Gianna's behavior as we left the states. I'm overjoyed that we'll be parents and my face is lit up with a huge smile and Jaime looks uncertain. I express my joy at the news of our impending bundle of joy, and embrace her, both of us turning to Jaime, who has remained silent.

"Jaime, please say something. Your silence concerns me."

Jaime looks back at us. "I'm happy, just shocked at how fast this has happened. If I'm being honest, I'm a little scared for us to have a baby and what will my role be? Are we ready to have a baby?"

Jaime looks at us with a concerned expression and Gianna sits on her lap and hugs her "you will be mama and I will be mommy and we will treat this baby as if it is all of ours. I know the timing is a bit off, but birth control isn't 100% and I think we are as ready as we'll ever be to be parents."

Jaime hugs her back and I stand behind the chair. "When we get back, we can find an OBGYN and then look at telling our families we're expecting."

They both look up at me. "You know you aren't supposed to announce a pregnancy until 12weeks?"

Gianna and I look at Jaime with a confused expression. "What I paid attention in health class." We laugh and prepare for bed, filled with excitement.

Gianna has programmed the alarm for 10am the following morning to ensure that everyone could wake up in good time and be ready for the day. When we woke, Gianna's absence from the bed was apparent and the aroma of cooking wafted through the air, likely her doing. She had made provisions for us to have a chef for the duration of our stay in Spain so that we can enjoy our vacation. Jaime and I prepare for the day by showering, and I am dressed in a T-shirt and shorts and Jaime is wearing a strapless, red summer dress with her blonde hair tied back in a ponytail. We head downstairs to see Gianna setting the table along with Jaime's 2 teenage nephews and I see Jaime's sister-in-law assisting the chef in plating the food. Music is playing in the background, and everyone is talking. As soon as we show up, we greet everyone and then lend a helping hand wherever needed. The rest of Jaime's family comes down a few minutes after we did. We eat breakfast and the cleaning crew begins their work, and we follow Gianna outside to be greeted with a bus big enough to fit everyone and we head to the first adventure of the day.

Jaime

This trip was absolutely amazing and I can't think Gianna or Luca enough for planning this. We spent the last three weeks exploring Spain and getting to know my family better. This trip has allowed me to get closer to my father and my brothers and their families. I wasn't able to attend my brother's weddings due to not having the finances to make it, so I wasn't able to get to know my sister-in-law. This trip gave us the opportunity to talk, and we found out we had a lot in common than we knew. To celebrate the last day of the trip, Gianna had organized a graduation gathering with my father and my brothers' families. I had a conversation with my father at the graduation party concerning his relationship with my mother. I attempt to gain a more thorough understanding of my father's place with my mother and possibly even implore him to move forward and let it go. My father has clung to the notion that he and my mother will reunite, thus blocking him from searching for love in Spain, as he is still stuck on her. I find it unjust that my father remains fixated on my mother while she has multiple intimate partners and expresses her displeasure whenever he has a new special someone. We discussed my therapy sessions, and my father was receptive as we talked about how his actions influenced my childhood.

He seemed like he was open to listening to me, and he finally said sorry for everything I had to go through when I was younger. He said if he could do it again, he wouldn't have sold drugs. During the party, I spotted Luca talking to my brothers and they seem to get along well, and I see them laughing and joking around and it makes me feel happy. Honestly, this trip is what I required to help mend my relationship with my father and my siblings' relationships. I'm aware my mother will have something to say when I return to the states, yet truthfully, I'm at the point where I don't worry about her opinion and if she has an issue, then it's her own issue and I'm no longer going to pacify her. My mother's behavior of control and persuasion has had a tremendous impact on my life, and I don't intend to let it continue in this manner; our relationship will now be different. I'm no longer the only one I have to consider; I need to look out for Luca and Gianna, as well as the new baby on the way. Therapy has provided me with the courage to set limits regarding my relationships with my parents and not to continue with the same behaviors I had in the past. I now realize that I am on the path to healing some of my childhood traumas and bettering my relationships with people.

The morning of when we leave, we all get packed up and my brother their families, my father Luca and Gianna and I all get into the sprinter van and head to the airport. Our flights are close together and it's a bittersweet feeling that we have to part ways so soon, though we have agreed to make plans for another trip together. The flight back to Seattle was long, but we were glad to be heading back. On the plane ride, we discussed matters including the baby and what the next steps were mainly concerning moving into the new home. We have settled on a home in Point Defiance with four rooms, and an expansive backyard, which should accommodate our growing family. We talked about the commitment ceremony that we will have at the beginning of fall. We wanted to have the ceremony before the baby is born and we also had a conversation about additional kids. We have spoken about children in the past, but we never went back to the conversation. We have decided that we wanted to have a minimum of three or four children and we wanted to have a three-year gap between them. When the plane touched down, a ride was waiting for us to take us to Lucas's apartment. After the lengthy flight, we arrived late in the night and were so worn out that we changed into our pajamas and conked out as soon as we were in. The sudden time changes threw our body clocks off balance, and when we awoke the following day, it was 1:00 PM on a Saturday. I helped Luca in cooking brunch and Gianna perched on the couch while talking with the realtor and finding an OBGYN and setting up an appointment. After our late brunch, we all went our own ways; I contacted my mother to tell her about my trip. My mother's phone rings two or three times, and she picks up. "Oh, look, it's my daughter who calls after three weeks of ignoring me? " I roll my eyes. Of course, she's going to start off with this because of our extensive plans during the trip. I only texted my mother and called her maybe once.

"Hello mother, how are you? I'm doing fine. What have you been up to? That's how proper greeting would've gone."

"Maybe my daughter would have gotten a proper greeting if she called me during her trip and did not ignore me."

I'm sitting on the couch rubbing my temples, understanding that this conversation has gone downhill and contemplating whether I wanted to continue speaking to her. Defying my judgement, I remain on the call in the hopes my mother displays maturity.

"I had an enjoyable experience with my dad and siblings. I formed a closer relationship with my sister-in-laws, nieces and nephews during the trip, and Gianna was so kind to give me a second graduation celebration."

The line gets quiet. "Seemed like you had a great time with your dad and siblings. I always tried to make sure your brothers were around, but their mom was always mad that your dad picked me. That woman was so hostile, I avoided her. I'd always advise keeping your distance because they got that bitter woman's genes."

My eyes roll. "You know speaking ill of their mother doesn't do you any favors. Suggesting my brothers are a danger to me is taking it too far. You never tried to build a bond with them when you were with dad. Maybe the bitter one wasn't their mother, but you."

I hear a gasp on the other line, and I picture my mother clutching her chest. "Why are you taking her side? Their mom called me names and tried to ruin Dad and me when we were married, so you shouldn't be standing up for her. You should stand up for your mom."

"I'm not sticking up for their mom. I'm just saying that speaking badly of her doesn't look good on you, either. I'm also defending my brothers because they didn't have a choice in how they came into the world, but you will show them respect when you talk to me." I hear sniffling. Oh brother, here come the tears.

"You visit your dad's family and now you're being disrespectful to the person who took care of you all those years. Especially after all the stuff he's put us through. I've been taking care of you since he left, and now you're standing up for him and his kids. You really disappointed me. When you come to your senses, let me know."

The line went dead, and I wasn't in the mood to call her back and put up with her immature behavior. Going to therapy's taught me that if I don't put a stop to my mom's behavior, she'll keep running my life. I need to draw the line and let her know that this isn't okay, and my therapist said to let her come back to me, not me going after her. I discussed with my therapist how I thought that would be rude, and she said respect is a two-way street. My mom needs to show me respect and not cross my boundaries. If she tries to manipulate me, I have to call her out and make it clear she can't do that.

Me: *I* don't appreciate you hanging up on me. You're trying to make me agree with your immature ideas and I'm not having it. If you want to talk like adults, call me once you've calmed down. I love you and hope to speak to you soon. That text message got an immediate response from my mom.

Mami: Have you lost your ever-loving mind, little girl? Don't you ever speak to me like that. I swear I don't know where your disrespect has come from, but you need to lose it real quick. You won't be hearing from me until you apologize for that rude text to your mom. If that means we don't talk for a bit, then ok, come to me when you find your respect. Have a good night.

Tears form in my eyes. All I wanted to do was have a normal conversation with my mother and tell her about my trip. She became melodramatic and unreasonable and now she is making me feel bad for standing by my boundaries. I just want my mother to respect me and treat me like an adult and not some puppet she can manipulate. I get up and search for either Luca or Gianna and I find Gianna sleeping in bed and, not wanting to disturb her. I close the bedroom door and look for Luca. I located Luca in the office, and I perched myself on the chair in front of his desk.

He lifts his head from his paperwork. "Are you all right, Jaime?"

When he uttered those words, my eyes filled with tears, and he rose to his feet and walked over to me, gathering me into his arms and taking me to the sofa. As I sob into his shoulder, he asks, "Is it your mother?"

I shake my head yes and he lets a sigh of frustration. "It pisses me off she keeps treating you as a child and demanding you obey her every command. Seamus and I were ecstatic when you left her household and put some distance between y'all. I remember the fight you had with her when you told her you were moving. She wanted you to stay another year so you could assist with bills, not considering you wanted to have your own place."

I continue to have my head buried in his shoulder. I remember that day and the following days where she denied my calls and didn't attend my housewarming. Only after I came to her and apologized for moving out did she talk to me again. Now that I think about it, it was ridiculous, and there's no need for me to apologize since she messed up.

Gaining my composure "I don't want to talk with my mother for a while until she can apologize to me this time. It's time I set this boundary and stick to it once and for all." We spent the rest of the night hugging and cuddling until we finally got ready for bed and snuggled up with Gianna.

Gianna

July

I am currently sitting on the couch, looking over the plans for the move and the commitment ceremony. Together, we have put a lot of effort into planning the ceremony events during the last three weeks. Aniyah got engaged to Seamus, and I helped Seamus get the restaurant booked for the two of them. Seamus initially told Luca that he did not need any help with organizing the engagement, however, he eventually sent me a text message when he had difficulty with putting together his plan. Assisting Seamus in planning the engagement for Aniyah was something I was more than happy to do, as he is the man she always deserved. When Aniyah announced she was pregnant with twins shortly before she was to be engaged, she was further along than I was, so I could tell her my pregnancy news and she agreed to keep it a secret from Seamus until I was ready to share.

The first few weeks of July were going to be chaotic because of multiple events happening at one time. Luca, Jaime, and I are moving into our new home within the next three days and our commitment ceremony will take place this Friday on July 8th. Seamus mentioned Java Books will open July 15th and they're hoping to be in their new home before that. Glancing at the calendar, I'm surprised how close we are to having it all planned. Life sure has a way of surprising us. It's all so well arranged that Seamus and Luca's parents can go to both events with no issues. I found room for my OBGYN appt in between all the events, and Luca and Jaime rearranged their days. Going over the list of guests for the commitment ceremony, I'm double-checking that we invited everyone we wanted. Jaime and her mom were still not on good terms, but Jaime still wanted her mother at the ceremony, so she didn't have any remorse. Her mom said yes to the invite and I'm hoping it'll mean an apology and them patching things up. Ceremony's good to go and the move's all good - checked off my list.

Jaime and Luca come home. We grab dinner and talk about what's coming up, then go off to bed. The house move was easier than expected. The movers were right on schedule and started putting the boxes into the van. "Unbelievable. I'm saying goodbye to my bachelor pad and hello to our family home." Luca was checking out his empty living room when Jaime and I joined him and hugged him. We're starting a new family chapter and ending this one. Glancing around, I start to tear up. I've only been in this condo for a short time, but it's already made an enormous impact on me. I'm so thankful for all the good times I've had here. When we get in the elevator, we observe the door shutting for the last time, signifying our departure from the place that has helped us to develop.

LUCA

On the morning of my commitment ceremony, I am gazing at my reflection in the mirror, surrounded by Jaime's siblings, Seamus, my dad, and Gianna's dad. Right now, all I can think of is that today's the start of the rest of my life. Jaime and Gianna breathed life into my mundane existence.

Seamus comes behind me and clasps my back. "Look at us man, who would've thought our year would entail both of us becoming husbands and next step fatherhood."

He goes to the liquor cabinet and takes out Guinness and opens a bottle for me and everyone else and passes the bottles around. "Let's raise our glasses to Jaime, Luca, and Gianna's future. May their dreams be fulfilled and may god look after their future family.

Everyone raises their bottles "Cheers!" The day of wedding planner comes to the room and tells everyone to get ready.

The ceremony is about to begin, and everyone files out except my dad. "Son, I want to say I am proud of all you have accomplished and what you will accomplish. I have always regarded you as my son, and when your mother and I adopted you, our family felt complete. I love you with all my heart."

I was crying and my dad held me in an enormous hug. I let him embrace me and the planner said something else before we went downstairs to the arch.

I am standing under the ceremony arch, and I survey the outdoor venue and see everyone that we love here to celebrate our love. The music plays and Gianna comes down the aisle first with her father dressed in a lace princess style wedding dress with a lace veil to match. Tears are forming in my eyes again, and Gianna's father places her hand on mine. Once Gianna's dad was seated, the music kept going, and Jaime came down with a surprise: her mom was on one side and Eduardo on the other. Jaime's wearing a cream jumpsuit and a cape over her shoulders. Jaime and her mom's eyes are red. It looks like they're trying to fix things. Her mother interlocked Jaime's hand with Gianna's and mine and gave a nod of approval, which made me smile in delight, as the only thing I desired for Jaime was to have a strong bond with her mother. The ceremony was a success, more than I ever dreamed of, and when it was done, everyone was in tears.

We were taking wedding photos when Gianna pulled Jaime and me to the side. "I want to announce the pregnancy at the reception."

We look at her and Jaime chimes in, "if you are ready to announce then we will stand by you."

"I agree with Jaime. If you are ready, then we are ready too."

"I think it's time we let our families know I'm 8 weeks now and I'm okay with everybody knowing. And Jaime, don't act like we won't chat about you walking down the aisle with your mom. What happened?"

Jaime looks at the both of us. "While I was in the bridal suite getting ready, she came and knocked on the door. I told her I wasn't up for talking, scared she'd start another fight before the wedding. She finally apologized for what she did to me. She had time to think, and she spoke with my aunt and my aunt called her out for her behavior. My mom realized she had turned into her mom, and she wasn't happy about it, since she and her mom hadn't talked for years before she passed away. Even on my grandmother's deathbed, she never apologized for the trauma she has caused my mother and her sisters. She said she didn't want to repeat history and honestly, that was the best thing she ever has done for me."

She had tears forming in her eyes, and Gianna and I formed a circle and hugged her. "This is truly the start of the rest of our lives," looking at my wives I respond,

"I can't agree more with Gianna."

Seamus came by to tell us everyone was looking for us, so we headed to the reception area and got a round of applause. As soon as we were seated, our friends and family came to congratulate us, and we figured we'd do our first dance. It was complicated, but we made it work with Jaime in the middle and Gianna and me around her. Afterwards, we all danced with our parents and Jaime's dad was on Zoom on a tablet. Jaime danced with him while holding the tablet close. Gianna and I gave each other a look, and I got the crowd's attention by tapping my glass.

"First off, thanks to everyone who showed up to celebrate with us. We have an announcement to make!"

I let Gianna take the floor and Jaime stood between Gianna and me. "We wanted to let you know we're expecting a baby and are due in February!"

Before she could finish, the room erupted in cheers and people surrounded us to give us more congratulations.

Seamus wraps his arms around my shoulders. "Looks like we're both going to be on this fatherhood journey together."

I shove Seamus and laugh and walk around the reception and a familiar face catches my attention. "Hillary, it's been a while. How are you feeling? ,"

She faces me and I see she has a date with her. "Luca, congratulations again and I am doing so much better. I have been on medication and going to therapy and I even accepted a job at the homeless shelter I used to volunteer at. Also, this is my boyfriend, Frank. we met at a conference in Arizona. He works at a shelter in Portland."

Frank smiles and holds out his hand and I take it and shake it. I assume her invitation was Jaime and Gianna's doing, and I am glad that they did. She looks more like the Hillary I first hired.

"I am so glad that you are doing so much better. I wish you and Frank the best and if you need anything, don't feel afraid to reach out.,"

She grins at me. "I can't think all of you for what you have done for me. You guys helped me at my lowest point and if you guys need anything. My number is still the same." She and frank walk away, I presume to find Gianna or Jaime.

We partied all night, and we stayed at a honeymoon suite at a hotel close by. The suite's got a roomy living room, a doorway to the bedroom, plus a pail of sparkling cider and chocolate-dipped strawberries. Jaime opens the bottle and pours three glasses and hands it to us "cheers to our family." We clink glasses and drink. We spend the rest of the night making love and laying in each other's arms, soaking in the happiest moment of our lives. The sun shines in through the blinds and I see Gianna is awake in a bathrobe standing on the balcony. I throw on my pajama pants that are lying next to the bed and join her on the balcony. It's a cool July morning and I come behind her and wrap my hands around her waist and place a hand on her belly. I'm the luckiest woman around to have two loves.

I gave her a kiss on the cheek. "Marriage and a kid weren't in my plans this year, but I'm glad destiny brought us together."

We hear the door open, and Jaime comes out wearing my dress shirt from last night buttoned up. "What are y'all doing out here?"

Gianna looks back at her and grabs her belly. "Just thinking how lucky we are to have this life."

Jamie comes over and places her hand on Gianna's belly. "Yea, we are pretty lucky, and I can't wait to meet this little peanut in February." I hug Jaime and Gianna and we watch the sun come up over the trees.

Jaime

The days after the wedding were a blur of activity as we helped Seamus and Aniyah move into their new home and attend Seamus's literary café opening. Gianna was incredible and got all the boxes unpacked in the new home, plus she made a list of what we needed for the other rooms. We all voted on what we'd keep and donate from both Luca's and my places. Gianna has been hanging out with Nova a lot and has been staying over at our house now that her mom's cool with it. Mattea had a meetup with Gianna's parents, and she gave them the okay to take Nova to Italy for a couple of weeks this month. We couldn't accept her parents' invite because of our schedules. Nova said that even though her parents are splitting up, her dad, who she grew up with, still wants to stay connected. We were all concerned about Nova's relationship with him after the divorce, so I'm glad she's still in contact. I am sitting at my desk looking over the recent numbers and I hear a notification and I check my phone and see a text from Gianna.

Gianna: *So help settle a debate between Luca and me. I think the baby's room should be in the room right next to us and Luca thinks the baby's room should be the down the hall from us. What do you think?*

Me: *We can have the baby room be right next to us and when the baby becomes a toddler, we can move the baby's room down the hall.* I heard another notification, and I saw Gianna screenshot the text and put it in the group chat. They are currently going back and forth, and I laugh at the responses.

Me: *Gianna, when is your OBGYN appointment again?*

Gianna: *It's this Friday. Are you guys still going to make it?*

Luca: *We will make it and this conversation isn't over. We still need to vote as a family.*

When the clock hits 5:30, I wait at the door to walk out with Luca. Due to us moving in together, we found it cost-effective to drive in together. Also, because my car being older than Gianna and Luca's we sold it and put the money from the sale into a savings account for the baby.

I am sitting in the building's lobby when I receive a call from my mom, and I pick up "Hey mama, what's up?"

"Hey Mija, I wanted to let you know first but your father and I have tried a relationship one more time,"

I look at my phone "um do you really think that is a smart decision considering you are in the states, and he is in Edinburgh?"

"That's something else I wanted to speak about you know I am retiring within the next month and I'm considering moving to Edinburgh to retire."

My mind is whirling and even though I am happy my parents are getting back together; I am not sure if it's healthy for either of them to be together. "I want to be happy you and papa are getting back together, but do you think you guys are in the right frame of mind to be in a relationship with each other?"

"We've been doing couple's counseling together for the past two months and I am not moving until September to give time for my visa to go through. Also, I have been doing independent therapy as well, which has been helping"

Tears form in my eyes and I am beyond proud of my parents for starting therapy. "Did I hear you correctly? You're in therapy? My mother in therapy?"

My mom chuckles. "Yes, after speaking with your aunt, I realized I have some work I need to do. I don't want to be like my mother and it's never too late to get therapy."

"I'm proud of you, mama for getting therapy and making progress. I love you and I support you."

I see Luca coming into the lobby. "Thank you Mija, I love you too."

I hang up the phone and Luca has a questionable look on his face "my mom is going through therapy and she and my father are getting back together"

We walk to the car "I'm happy she's going through therapy but is it a good thing your mom and dad are getting back together."

"We'll see."

We get in the car and head home and as soon as we enter, we smell something good. "I'm in the kitchen cooking." I took my shoes off and placed my purse by the hook near the garage door.

I walked through the living room to see Gianna in the kitchen. When we were house shopping, Gianna wanted an open kitchen. Gianna did the bulk of the cooking, so Luca and I agreed without a fuss.

I walk behind Gianna and stand on my tippy toes to give her a kiss on the cheek. "Watcha cooking good looking?"

She laughs. "I'm cooking a one pot chicken and vegetable skillet recipe. I didn't feel like dirtying up a lot of dishes."

Luca is sitting on the couch with a Guinness in his hand. "It smells good."

I started getting the table ready and when we sat down, I filled Gianna in on what happened with my parents and that they're going to counseling. She was ecstatic that my parents were getting help and giving love another go. We spent the rest of the night watching Netflix and cuddling on the couch.

Gianna

December

My due date's almost here and we found out a few months back it's a boy. Gianna already had twins, and we've been visiting her as much as possible since my pregnancy almost finished. We chatted about how our babies would be more than just cousins, but best friends, too. For Thanksgiving, we went to Jaime's mum in Edinburgh, and she and Jaime's dad were engaged. They're doing well and it makes Jaime happy to see her parents healing from past trauma. We flew to Canada for Jesse's wedding to her high school sweetheart. In a week, we are flying to Ireland to spend time with Seamus's parents and family. They are renting an enormous house and invited most of their family to stay. My doctor gave me the clear to travel for Christmas. Had a few rough moments in my pregnancy, but other than that I'm loving it. I even joked to Jaime and Luca that I wouldn't mind getting pregnant sooner than the 3-year limit we set.

I am in the nursery with Nova, who is helping me organize the nursery. She has been beyond helpful during this pregnancy and is excited to have a cousin.

I'm in the rocker folding laundry when Nova looks at me and says, "you think my dad would've been a good dad?"

I stop rocking. Nova has asked about Fabiano, but she doesn't bring him up as much as she did when she first came into the family. "I can't say if he would've been a good dad, but I know he was my best friend while he was here. At night he'd read me stories, play with me and my dolls, and teach me to ride my bike. Fabiano had a lot of demons and if he had the help he required, he could've been a good dad."

She looks at me with tears forming in her eyes. "thank you for the honest answer. A part of me is sad that I will never get to know him, but I am also glad that he isn't suffering anymore, and I like to think he's in a better place."

I open my arms and she come over to hug me. "have I told you how I am glad that you are comfortable talking about your emotions? You know me, your mom, dad and grandparents are all here if you ever need to talk to someone."

We hear the garage door open. "I know I am lucky to have so many people who love me and look out for me."

Jaime calls up the steps. "I'm making dinner. Is Nova staying for dinner?"

Nova yells down, "yes ma'am thank you." We have a wonderful family dinner and Luca takes her home afterwards.

As I'm heading to bed, I see Luca coming out of the bathroom with his muscles on display, wearing his lounge pants. My pregnancy hormones kick in overdrive, and I bite my lip and Luca catches me. He climbs onto the bed and kisses me, and I feel wetness forming between my legs. "Are you needy, my lovely wife?" I nod my head and Luca grabs the bottom of the long shirt I am wearing and lifts it above my head to take it off. He then removes my panties and begins kissing my thighs. He then reaches my pussy and sucks on my clit in a gentle rhythm until I orgasm. The shower stops and Jaime comes out without a towel and even after orgasming, I get wet all over again. Jaime joins us in the bed and kisses me, then Seamus. My stomach's getting in the way, but Jaime went down on me, and Seamus is getting in from behind. We spent the night making love then cuddling.

A week passes, and before I know it is time to leave for Ireland. The night before we leave for the flight is chaotic as always and somehow, we all get to the private airport hangar in time for the flight. The Gallagher's have rented out a private airplane and we are riding with Luca and Seamus's parents, Seamus, Aniyah and the twins, Alana, and Aiden. Mrs. Gallagher shocked Aniyah by inviting her family to fly with us, and she loved it. We left at 7:15 am; it was a long flight with a stopover, and we finally arrived in Ireland at 8 the next morning. We had a sprinter van waiting for us and to our surprise, when we got to the villa, my parents and Nova were there along with Jaime's parents and brothers and their families.

In Ireland, Luca and Seamus gave us ladies the grand tour of the places they visited as kids. Seamus, Aniyah, and the kids parted ways after dinner at a delightful spot by the water. Luca's been acting strange recently and he eventually let Jaime and me in on why. Before the trip, he was looking into his biological parents and wrote them letters - his dad didn't answer but his mom did. He intended to see her in jail while we were there, and Jaime and I joined him. Luca could get some answers and voice what he was feeling. His mom apologized for all she had done and, by the end of the meeting, said he could keep writing if he wanted. Christmas was such a blast, and everyone was so happy for Alana and Aiden's first Christmas. I looked around and noticed how different this year ended compared to how it started.

Luca

After New Year's things at work started getting busy as most people were getting back into it now that the holidays were done.

I am sitting at my desk looking over paperwork when Jasmine knocks on the door. "Come in."

Jasmine enters with a worried expression on her face. "Jasmine, I don't like that face. What's wrong?"

She comes in with paperwork. "Remember that subsidiary that went belly up last year that we combined with our other subsidiary?"

I raise an eyebrow. "Yes, the one that it took us months to work out a plan that worked for everyone. What about it?"

She takes a seat in front of me. "Not what you want to hear, but I think we should push the board to get rid of the CO-CEO. The CEO's accusing the Co-CEO of bad financial decisions that could put the company in danger."

I groan and a migraine forms. "Do you think we have the votes to do so?"

She hands me a folder with communications with the board. "I have been speaking with board members who are equally concerned with the CO-CEO decisions and want to oust him before he does damage."

I read over the documentation, and she is right. The board wants him out "set up a vote within the next week but don't tip off the CO-CEO so he doesn't lobby the board and try to stop the vote."

She nods and heads out of my office and I order lunch at the carryout down the street and order Jaime's lunch and send her a text message telling her I placed an order.

The day is finally done, and Jaime is driving us home as we are chatting about our day. Gianna calls, and it usually means she has a pregnancy craving.

I pick up "hi honey, Jaime and I are on our way home. Would you like us to pick something up on the way in?" I hear deep breaths on the other line. "Honey are you okay?"

She answers "yes and no, my water broke, and the contractions are coming. Where are you guys?"

That gets me alert and I put her on speaker "we just came over by the Safeway by N pearl St. What is the time between contractions?" Jaime perks up.

"My contractions are 10 minutes apart and they last about a minute."

Jaime steps on the gas and through her speeding we make it home in record time and I stay on the phone until we arrive home. We get out and run up the steps and see Gianna sitting on the couch deep breathing. Jaime runs to her and I run to the room to get the go bag and I come down as Jaime is walking her through the breathing exercise we learned in Lamaze classes.

Through her breathing "call...my...parents" and I run back to the car and grab my phone.

I dial her mother, and she picks up on the second ring. "Hey Luca, what's up?"

"Mrs. Guzzo Gianna is in labor. Her contractions are 10 minutes apart."

She doesn't say anything I hear her calling for her husband. "how are her contractions?"

I hear drawers opening. I look over and Gianna is still trying to take deep breaths. "she's taking it like a champ. It looks like she isn't in any major pain." I walk to the kitchen and I feel something hit the back of my head and I turn around to see a slipper near me. "What was that for? I just said that you looked like you weren't in any pain."

She gives me death glare and Mrs. Guzzo says "Luca, sweetie, don't continue. Also, we are going to be on the first flight out."

I sit by Gianna and Jaime, helping her as much as I can as we wait for our baby boy.

Jaime

After around 5 hours helping Gianna, she's ready for the hospital. Gianna's parents showed up, and Seamus's parents were nice enough to give them a ride to our house. Seamus and Aniyah showed up at the hospital and luckily got a sitter for the babies. As I watched them prepare Gianna for labor, I became overwhelmed. Our little boy's about to arrive and we finally picked a name while we were at home. We all agrees on Jonathan Fabiano Gallagher: I chose Jonathan because it means 'gift from God' in the Bible. Gianna wanted to give the baby her brother's name as a way of honoring him, and Jonathan would have Luca's last name.

I step out of the room for a minute to call my mom and she picks up "hi mija what's up?"

"Gianna is in labor and we are going to have our baby boy"

I hear a gasp. "Your dad and I will try to make it out there as soon as possible"

My mother is about to hang up when I say "wait."

"Yes is there something else"

"yes mom I am scared what if I end up being a bad mom and repeat the generational mistakes that I have been trying to fix?"

"Jaime I think you are going to be the best mom you know why?"

"Why?"

"You broke the cycle by going to therapy and admitting you needed help. Your dad and I spent our lives ignoring our own pain and repeating the same mistakes our parents made. You had to be a parent when you should have been a kid, so you've got this mom thing down for sure. I love you with all my heart. You got this." She hangs up and I'm in tears. My mom gave me the motivation I needed, and I inhaled deeply before going back to see my son come into the world.

Gianna went through 8 hours of labor and our baby boy arrived- 7 pounds, 2 ounces and 19 inches long. He's the cutest baby ever, and we're all crying, and I kissed Gianna and Luca. Luca and I cut the umbilical cord and gave the nurse his name and the three of us went to hold him and do chest to chest.

Luca's carrying the baby and I'm glancing at Gianna. "you did a good job mama"

I kiss her forehead again "hey I am supposed to be mommy you are mama" we laugh a little and watch Luca bond with our son. The nurses took Jonathan to make sure he was fit, and then they monitored Gianna and Luca went to the lobby to make the announcement. We chatted with our families while the nurses got our baby, and our families got to meet him, excluding my parents from Edinburgh. Life is great.

EPILOUGE

Gianna
6 years later

This morning is chaos magnified. I am holding Elizabeth, one of our 4-year-old twins, while running to catch Jonathan to get him dressed for his first day of school. I hear Luca in the twins' room getting Emmanuel dressed and just when

Jonathan rounds the corner, a very pregnant Jaime stops him and scoops him up. "When mommy tells you to come here, you don't run. Let's take you back to your room to get dressed, but first say sorry to mommy."

Jonathan looks up at me with his hazel eyes and curly reddish-brown hair "sorry mommy."

Jaime puts Jonathan down and he heads to his room. Jaime holds out her hand.

I hand her Elizabeth. "I will get Lizzy dressed. Go take care of Jonathan."

I kissed her belly and rubbed it - we initially agrees three would be enough, but after I had the twins, we wanted one more. Since I was at risk for a high-risk pregnancy post with the twins, Jaime was the one to carry the last one. I head to Jonathan's room, who is still in his Iron Man pajamas, and he is sitting on the bed. I help him pick out clothes for the first day of school.

Luca

I am finishing getting Emmanuel dressed when I hear the door open and see Jaime carrying Elizabeth in. Emmanuel runs over to Jaime to hug her leg and attempt to climb her.

I grabbed Elizabeth. "I can get her dressed. Can you get breakfast ready for everyone?"

She smiles at me. "Yes, I can. Gianna is getting Jonathan ready. Do you want to come downstairs and help mama with breakfast?"

Emmanuel grins and shakes his head and runs ahead of Jaime. I moved the office from Auburn to Tacoma a few years ago, and everyone was really excited since the commute was much shorter. Moving has been beneficial because after going to Jonathan's first day at kindergarten, Jaime and I will go into the office and the commute is 10 minutes. The office is just 11 minutes from the house and Jonathan's school. In case of an emergency, either of us can get to Jonathan.

I'm carrying Elizabeth as I go down and Jaime and Emmanuel have the table set and Gianna and Jonathan are behind. We have breakfast as a family, buckle the kids in and head out to elementary school. I snagged a great parking spot, and we hopped out to take shots with Jonathan. Jonathan was surprised when Nova, Seamus, and Aniyah, our parents, showed up. Seamus and Aniyah's twins started school before Jonathan, and we could see them off and they came down to see Jonathan off. When it came time to say goodbye, it was hard as Jonathan clung to us and cried.

I picked him up. "What's with the tears, little man?"

Jonathan tells me through his tears, "I don't want you, mama or mommy to leave."

I wipe his eyes. "I know, but you have to be a big boy for us and go to school. We will be here after school to pick you up and if you are a big boy, I will take you to Frisco Freeze for a burger and milkshake."

That perks him up. "Okay, I can be a big boy."He gave me a hug, then I sat him down and he went to his classroom. Jaime and Gianna are holding the twins and they are crying as well and they are being comforted by our families. Me and my wives headed back to the car to get the twins buckled up. We said goodbye to our families and both Jaime and Gianna's parents told us they will see us tonight.

I walked over to speak with Seamus. "I can't believe our babies are growing up."

Seamus looks at me. "Yea, it feels like just yesterday they were babies and now look at them. After this new baby Aniyah and I talked about me getting a vasectomy. We think 4 is enough."

I chuckles. "Yeah, I think we're going to stop at 4 as well. Are we still meeting up this weekend in Seattle for a play date?"

"Yes, we are. Aniyah was thinking about taking the kids to the Space Needle."

"I think that's fine. I'll talk with Gianna to verify you know she is the family planner."

We chuckle and observed our wives and Nova talking. Jaime rubs Aniyah's belly and vice versa.

I turn back to Seamus, "I hear Nadia is getting signed with the Seattle Storm."

He smiles. "Potentially Aniyah says there's still contract negotiations I'll let you know about any updates. I hear Nova is enjoying UW Seattle and Aniyah mentioned she is being pursued by a Seattle Mariners player."

I raise an eyebrow. "Yea, but I'm not sure it'll turn into anything." We talk for a few more minutes before we all leave the parking lot. As I take Gianna and the twins' home, Gianna takes my hands in hers. "This life is such a blessing. Our relationship was unconventional, but I wouldn't want it any other way." I reflect and I am in complete agreement.

GIANNA

JAIME

LUCA

Don't miss out!

Visit the website below and you can sign up to receive emails whenever Brianne Turner publishes a new book. There's no charge and no obligation.

https://books2read.com/r/B-A-UQREB-AQFED

Connecting independent readers to independent writers.

Also by Brianne Turner

The Lost African Princess
The Lost African Princess: The Prequel

Standalone
An Unconventional Love Affair

Watch for more at https://authorbrianneturner.com.

About the Author

Brianne's love for reading started at a young age and has grown over the years. Her passion for reading fueled her creativity inspiring her to write short stories. It was only recently that she found her voice as an author and began sharing her stories with the world. Nesteled in the outskirts of Seattle she shares a home with her beloved fiance Ben and a an active tuxedo cat named TomTom.

Read more at https://authorbrianneturner.com.

9 798218 304416